PRAISE FOR GINA NUTT'S *NIGHT ROOMS*

"*Night Rooms* is vulnerable, cinematic, and positively transcendent. Gina Nutt uses themes and details from horror films as a way into a meditation on the deaths she's experienced in her own life, acting as a kind of literary final girl, asking, what does it mean to survive? Nutt's exploration of this question is captivating to read, as her chainsaw-sharp sentences carve a path toward the truth. I love this book."
—**Chelsea Hodson, author of *Tonight I'm Someone Else***

"Nutt navigates metaphor like an expert butcher—cutting and curing words until we're left with something totally new, a different animal than the original thought. A wonderful gift for anyone who has experienced loss, or an assault, any sort of violation that has guided them into their own night room."
—**Aimée Keeble, Main Street Books (Davidson, NC)**

"Gina Nutt uses horror movie tropes to weave together fragmented essays on anxiety and grief, homebuying, and shark-infused family vacations."
—**Eliza Smith, *Lit Hub* "Most Anticipated Books of 2021"**

"In this viscerally provocative collection of essays, life isn't so different from a horror movie—just be glad you have Gina Nutt as the Final Girl guiding you through. Whether through the lens of celebrating her wedding anniversary or competing in a beauty contest, Nutt relates the events of her life to the tropes in scary films, from haunted houses to slasher-induced gore. In writing both revelatory and intimate, Nutt probes the most frightening aspects of life in such a way that she manages to shed light and offer understanding even about those things that lurk in the deepest and darkest of shadows."
—**Kristin Iversen, *Refinery29***

Night Rooms

ESSAYS

GINA NUTT

Two Dollar Radio
Books too loud to ignore

Two Dollar Radio
Books too loud to Ignore

WHO WE ARE TWO DOLLAR RADIO is a family-run outfit dedicated to reaffirming the cultural and artistic spirit of the publishing industry. We aim to do this by presenting bold works of literary merit, each book, individually and collectively, providing a sonic progression that we believe to be too loud to ignore.

TwoDollarRadio.com

Proudly based in
Columbus
OHIO

 @TwoDollarRadio

 @TwoDollarRadio

 /TwoDollarRadio

Love the
PLANET?
So do we.

Printed on Rolland Enviro.
This paper contains 100% post-consumer fiber, is manufactured using renewable energy - Biogas and processed chlorine free.

Printed in Canada

100%

PCF

BIO GAS®
ENERGY

∞
PERMANENT

ISBN→ 9781953387004 : *Library of Congress Control Number available upon request.*

Also available as an Ebook.
E-ISBN→ 9781953387011 : *Book Club & Reader Guide* of questions and topics for discussion is available at twodollarradio.com

SOME RECOMMENDED LOCATIONS FOR READING *NIGHT ROOMS*:
Your favorite cemetery, park, or pumpkin patch. An indie movie theater, while waiting for the lights to dim. Or pretty much anywhere because books are portable and the perfect technology!

AUTHOR PHOTO→
David Nutt

COVER ART→
Woman in cell playing solitaire,
Nickolas Muray, circa 1950, Flickr

Excerpts from *Night Rooms* were published as the essay "The Four-Day Win" in *Cosmonauts Avenue*.

Night Rooms

1.

I used to imagine wanting someone alive would revive them, if caught right after dying. If I went after them, buoyed by reflexive hope, I might bring them back. Like losing something—a bracelet, a pair of sunglasses, a plastic sandal—over the side of a boat, seeing the outline dim as it sinks. I'd flood with instinct. Dive into the water right away, head first, to retrieve what was lost.

If I look at the sky at the right moment, evening and morning mirror each other—the light, the sky, the air's vague smell. A hazy line blurs the intervals, deepens my readiness to disorient myself, to lean deeper into dreams where I am falling and feel awake.

I have become acquainted with the creature feature: Life emerged from lake or sea, an isolated town, a gash in arctic ice. Ugly, ancient, miraculous. Some living thing scientists have not yet discovered. Some living thing scientists created, or found, and hid.

How body horror wrecks the human form: An infection, a botched experiment. The skin newly revised: a brilliant rash, cracking dryness, molted to accommodate a larger shape. Eyes bloodshot or jaundiced, blacked through by change. Pupils dilated wide, irises pressed into rings too thin to see. The spine, a seam where a costume zipper may hide.

I have watched rituals summon the supernatural and accidents awaken ghosts. Someone calls back from beyond the grave. Sometimes they take someone back with them.

Zombie and vampire films are familiar: Infectious bites and apocalypse templates. Eternal afterlife outlines for the undead. Survival strategies for the living.

Occasions for a slasher: Slumber party. Football game. Summer camp. Sorority. Cabin getaway. A too-perfect-to-be-real small town, often harboring secrets. A dream becomes a nightmare. First times. Making love in cars, on basement couches, living room couches, in the woods. Holidays and celebrations. Halloween, Christmas, Valentine's Day, birthdays, graduation, prom.

Events inspiring chainsaw massacres: Summer vacation, a road trip. A cannibal family living in a house of hoarded, dusty objects collected from victims. Almost everyone dies. Someone gets away in the end, but not really because the driver in the flagged-down car is a villain. Or the survivor goes to a hospital and when she stares out the window all she sees is a sunset and a fence, a man in a suit, tie, and white shirt. The man swings a chainsaw at the horizon. The blade splits the sky from the earth.

*

Someone noted as we walked around a city together that I ran across the crosswalk when the pedestrian light changed. *Scamper, scamper, scamper,* he sweetly teased. Breaking this habit is tough. My husband knows. He reassures me, *You don't have to run.*

Hands cupped as if asking for a communion wafer, I crept into the kitchen from the garage, approached my mother to show her what I'd found. The mouse was tiny and brown. The mouse was dead. I hadn't known. This is a story I have been told. I don't remember being there. Hearing a memory is like listening to someone describe a movie I can't remember seeing.

I remember the afternoon I set a butterfly in a doll house. The wings flickered and flattened, a black and orange mosaic like Halloween decorations laid in a box for storage. I ran the elevator, thinking one motion may inspire another, a domino effect, or seeing an object and finding the word to name it: plate, book, door. Whichever parent noticed may not have said *dead*, but this is as far back as I grasped the word uniting with the act. On its own, *dead* seemed inert and distant, different from understanding what it means to die, the feeling of being a witness.

The still wings unfolded a familiar fall in me. I sensed it watching a girl and her dog run from a funnel the sky focused on Kansas; an orange cat in a box floating down a river, missing his dog friend, listening to night sounds; a sea witch rising from ocean depths. I felt it when I saw night darken the golf course beyond the backyard and the photo of a bicycle found without a girl and her school picture in the newspaper; my parents warning someone could take me. The feeling may have been dread, a widening twinge, an ache I felt but could not name.

*

Some films suggest death is a temporary symptom relieved by waking. I remember Snow White in a glass casket, surrounded by forest animals gathered in collective mourn; Sleeping Beauty in bed, her hair fanned out on a white pillowcase. Movies about dream places seemed related. Dorothy carried by flying monkeys to a tower where she watches the red sand of her life nearly run out. This seemed tame compared to the sequel, in which Dorothy is admitted to a clinic for electrotherapy. A thunderstorm knocks out the power. A candy striper rescues her from the gurney. The girls run into woods beyond the clinic, a rushing river carries Dorothy back to Oz, which is in disrepair, populated with evil creatures. A princess steals heads to swap with her own, displaying her options in a hall of glass cases. She wakes one night to shattering, her headless frame rising from the mattress.

The in-between appealed to me. Pressing my cat's paws—the pink jellybean pads—against my closed eyelids, shapes and colors appearing. Swirls spun from blackness, circles and diamonds in pink, blue, and green. I liked how my body made that light.

*

The cartoon wolf movie is streaming this month. The birthday I turned eleven, my mother's boyfriend hauled sound and light equipment from work into our living room for my party. He spelled my nickname in neon light on the wall. I wore an outfit from Limited Too, my hair scrunchied in a ponytail. A boy with a bowl haircut gifted the cartoon wolf movie. I added the tape to my family's video shelves and didn't watch it. I still have it in a bin in my basement.

I worked for my English teacher during eighth-grade study hall, stapled packets and hole-punched worksheets to snap into three-ring binders. She brought me snowball snack cakes, marshmallow and pink-tinted coconut around chocolate crumb. The week the boy with the bowl haircut took his life, I arrived at study hall to work, instead of attending the wake with my classmates. My teacher seemed surprised. My mother may have called the wake morbid.

By then I knew about my great uncle's death. A principle dancer for the San Francisco ballet, he died by suicide during the company's 1969 run of *The Nutcracker*. I'd researched and written about him for projects and reports, because as a young girl I too was an aspiring ballet dancer. My grandmother, who was his sister, humored my interviews. I questioned whether all her stories were true—like the one in which my great uncle danced on a cable above the Golden Gate Bridge for a popular variety show. I craved a full picture of his inner weather. I wanted to hear something different and better understand. I wanted him alive for the brief spell earned when talking about someone who is dead.

*

I've heard each time a person remembers or shares a recollection, the mind archives the recall. The telling becomes a memory. New details emerge or sharpen, others blur or fade.

A Syracuse news clip from December 1986 shows a shopping mall, a movie theater marquee—titles, times, ratings. Lights aglow, framed film posters. The anchor describes a holiday boost in shopping and movie attendance: *Nat Tobin from USA Cinemas credits the surge in moviegoers to producers who are making a variety of movies that offer an alternative to what's already on cable and available for home video systems. So while producers may turn out more blockbusters, only time will tell if they'll be as successful as some of the old classics.*[1]

The anchor highlights forthcoming films. One clip shows a monstrous plant in a flower shop, belting a plea for human blood. The plant's stems and leaves wave, its giant puppet-mouth flaps.

Preference and context may influence a personal canon; the things we like matter as much as the things we experience, or the moment we see, or re-watch, a film.

I plug in my laptop, click on the TV. Repetition is not new. *Titanic*'s home video release came as two tapes. I watched so many times the VCR choked on the first one. My mother pried it out with a screwdriver.

I play something familiar, a movie or show I've already seen. I repeat seasons. I stopped counting how many times. I don't think I ever counted. I don't call this catharsis; it's closer to the feeling I get watching a slow-burn, how the movie expands my capacity for dread as it delays a jump scare or reveal.

In *Scream*, the horror nerd who works at the video store and drops genre tropes and rules throughout the movie says: *It's the millennium, motives are incidental.*[2]

I may say an intersection is not a sameness, movies aren't life, but a recognizable flicker, an event witnessed or experienced. A tape rewinds. The images replay. What fades? What is apparent this time? What did I miss before?

*

An index can obscure a feeling. A catalogue can footnote specificity. Both things can be true.

I once watched my brother spiral dish soap and water into a mixing bowl. He guided a wasp into the mixture and clapped a dinner plate over the top. I looked on, ready to run. My brother lifted the plate, revealed the wasp kicking in the soapy water. I felt a splash, a flutter, the bubbles in the frothy solution rupturing inside me.

The composer John Williams says of music in movies: *It's one of the beauties of the film medium that it's the combination of the visual and the situation—this being the shark or the knifing scene in Hitchcock's* Psycho—*combined with the notes; that combination of sound and image forming a memory.*[3]

A man approaches a beautiful woman in a mint-green bathtub in a vast, old hotel; a boy peers over the edge of his bed to gleeful laughter; a swimmer's legs kick through water, deep ocean-floor thumping, an orchestra accelerates. No matter how many times I watch these scenes, I still hold my breath. I may be waiting or hoping something different will happen.

I know another fin may appear on the horizon, my impulse to think *shark* when the fin could belong to a dolphin.

I used to imagine I'd get to say goodbye to everyone. I saw a serene, floral sleep, my hair on a satin pillow, many well-dressed mourners. I saw in what I watched. Context turned consequence. Prick a finger. Bite an apple. Get in the car, walk home alone, go in the room, go down the stairs, board the plane. Stay in bed and await an unseen funnel to swallow me. Go to sleep and forget: the stove, the deadbolt, how gas smells, which isn't how gas smells in its natural state, but mercaptan, an odorant added so dwellers recognize a leak by the smell of rotten eggs.

A woman or girl alive when a horror movie's credits roll joins an ancestry of women and girls who have done the same. They make a lineage of final girls. Each outlasted a struggle knowing she'd someday die, that anyone's immediate survival is only as urgent as the danger before them.

A rope split the shallow end from the deep. I sat on the diving board, kicking my toes in the water, while my brother cleaned the pool. I had on a blue jumper with a whale my mother painted on the front pocket. My brother swept the net through the water. He raised the skimmer, palmed a frog. Reaching for it, I fell in. My dress billowed around me. I saw the sky and sun clear through the water. I didn't think of swimming or drowning. The movements I learned in swim class were taught at the surface, my sinking happened below, too fast to pick a stroke. It almost didn't seem to be happening at all. I let myself fall back. Like action playing backward on a screen as a tape rewinds, slipping into the VCR's hum and whir.

If we attach ourselves to art, maybe art can attach itself to us. Do I find the movies or do they find me? I am making a lineage of what lingers. I am trying not to be afraid anymore.

2.

On a beach in the Outer Banks of North Carolina, a man stared at the Atlantic for a week. He built sandcastles with his grandchildren, ran each morning with one of his daughters. He went to an airplane museum.

Not many of us die from love or terror these days, and there are few thoughts left that touch us with true horror. But there are some, certainly. There's one. Earth's nightmare is the sea,[1] Joy Williams writes in her essay "Sharks and Suicide."

A photographer snapped the family on the beach at sunset. The men wore aqua-colored polo shirts and khaki shorts. The women wore white dresses. Thirteen smiling faces hovering above coordinated colors.

Who among us knows the extent of the sea's true abyss?[2]

The man knew this was the last family vacation everyone would take together before he died.

That a shore exists—even if its line doesn't cross the horizon—is not likely a comfort to someone swimming in the middle of the ocean.

The pressure exerted by the jaws of a typical eight-foot shark is three metric tons a square centimeter.//The shark is not in the tarot; it is not in the signs of heaven. Its strict reality remains beneath the waters of the world.[3]

A shark is a metaphor for unexpected death, as well as immense feeling, the sense of being tugged beneath the water.

Days, the man stared at the ocean with sunglasses over his eyes. Evenings, he mixed cocktails. If someone mentioned sand toys or sunscreen, the named object appeared on a granite kitchen counter within a few hours. He went to the store several times a day. Someone mentioned lobster at breakfast. The man bought frozen lobster tails, even though another dinner was planned.

No shark is seen in *Jaws* in the moment three men sit around a table after dinner, the boat's dark windows around their heads. Their excursion would be a leisurely fishing trip, if not for the monstrous shark swimming the water as they rock and bob in the night.

*

I lost my earrings in the ocean on the first day in the Outer Banks. I got a sunburn, my skin a pink flare on the sand. I waded, but did not swim out. I drifted on my back in the beach house pool. I feared sharks and whatever else swam the ocean, the wide horizon, all the ongoing water stretched out before me.

The ocean is balm and horror. Think of the surface, not the plunge beneath, the depths. Think of starfish, seahorses, dolphins, and sea lions, not sharks or deep-sea creatures.

One man searching for the rogue great white says:

Sometimes that shark, he looks right into you. Right into your eyes. You know, the thing about a shark, he's got lifeless eyes, black eyes, like a doll's eyes. When he comes at you, he doesn't seem to be living until he bites you, and those black eyes roll over white...[4]

I think of a shark going euphoric, delighted by a kill. Great white sharks lack a nictitating membrane, the protective inner eyelid that safeguards against the teeth or claws of struggling prey. They instinctively roll back their eyes in defense when they strike.

Horror has no shortage of sharks. They prowl the waters surrounding secluded beach houses. They circle unlucky swimmers stuck on rocks submerging beneath incoming tides. They orbit the deep voids of pristine gulfs. Supposedly extinct leviathan species emerge. They swim the sunk tunnels of ancient Mayan ruins. They flash horrible teeth in wild tornadoes.

More recent shark stars are punchlines as much as they are monsters. They don't strike the same fearful chords in me as *Jaws*; fear of monster, water, and void. The woman in the opening scene goes under on the first violent tug. Her head jerks back, her arms wave and thrash. Something pulls me down too.

*

At a birthday party in a pizza shop, a friend advises me grieving people exist in concentric rings—those closest to the dead are in the innermost ring, and so on. My father-in-law has just died. My friend tells me grieving people seeking support must lean only on rings outside their own. Which is to say, it is not advisable to lean forward on an inner circle of grief. If you are grieving you must lean on people in outward rings or you must lean into your own self.

13

Ithaca, New York, has several mottos. Local grocery store Wegmans devotes half an aisle to Ithaca-pride swag—tee shirts, hoodies, coffee mugs, license plate frames, bumper stickers, notebooks. One motto, often fondly cited: *Ten square miles surrounded by reality.*

It's a water city, too, thriving with creeks and lakes: Cayuga Lake, Six Mile Creek, Cayuga Inlet, Linderman Creek, Cascadilla Creek, Fall Creek, Beebe Lake. And plenty of waterfalls: Taughannock, Potter's, Wells, Ithaca, Cascadilla, Buttermilk, Lucifer.

Glaciers long ago raked through the region, left the gorges that inspired the city's namesake motto: *Ithaca is gorges.* Bridges sprawling the gouged earth are famous for epic views, notorious for people who have climbed over and let go. Following a cluster of suicides in 2010, temporary fences were installed on several bridges, with plans to implement more permanent barriers. Some community members argued the fences obstructed bridge views—a source of local pride and natural beauty—and someone intent on taking their life will find another way to do so. The long-term plan saw nets installed, extended from below the bridge decks, and the fences removed. I think of this struggle between place and people when I hear the square-mileage motto—a city surrounded by reality, but not part of it.

I lean into myself, rather than my outermost rings. I worry I'm spreading sadness, that hearing about suicide again and again is as jarring as another statement from local police about someone found in a gorge.

The assumption in a city with several colleges, one of which overlooks gorges, is that most people who jump are college students, but it's not true.

When I think of the green *Ithaca is gorges* tee shirt beside the *Ten square miles...* bumper sticker, I want to be the rail between the bridge and the gorge.

A misty early morning, a pink-edged sunset, stars dotting the night sky above the dark trees. I want to look without thinking of the drop below me. Even focusing on the horizon, vertigo splashes through me. The sensation is several temperatures at once and if I were to study them beneath a microscope, one by one, I might find each as fearful as the others—freezing despair, tepid ambivalence, glowing shame, a hopeless blaze capable of urging itself toward a dive.

*

Someone tells me the scene where a father takes his son to scream into a waterfall was filmed forty-five minutes away in Watkins Glen. I don't believe it, but I nod.

The city of Ithaca is not really ten, but 6.073 square miles.

A woman goes for a balletic swim. An aquatic creature swims beneath her, parallel to her. The creature reaches for the woman but does not touch her. The woman sinks beneath the surface to search the water. She senses something but she does not see it.

Drop an object into water and rings will expand from where it landed. Drop an object over the rail of a bridge spanning a gorge, you may not hear it hit the water, but I am trying to draw the rings. If the item dropped into water is a death, the ripples could be the people left behind, a map of the bereaved.

If life is temporary, why is the pain from losing someone to suicide so ongoing? Less like a creek or a lake, more like an ocean. The only horizon in sight an image that early explorers believed was the end of the world.

3.

My family sang along with the radio jingle on the car radio: *Going shopping at Camillus Mall. Things are hopping at Camillus Mall.* The mall was flat and sprawling, named for the suburb where it stood. Hardly aspirational or catchy, like Great Northern or ShoppingTown.

I walk the stage in the video, pose at each corner as the host reads my favorite foods, school subjects, and hobbies to the judges and audience. My eveningwear is from Easter mass, a floral print dress with fabric-covered buttons up the front. I wear a hat in the same bouquet, a pink rose pinning up the brim. My mother sewed my dress from beige Simplicity sheets. Gowns in royal-blue satin and seafoam-green tulle cross the stage. A sequined white bodice shimmers pink in the light, a stiff tulle skirt parallel to the ground, like a dancer's pancake tutu. The pageant host asks me to tell the audience about my pet. I'm so nervous, I fidget with my hands, as I'd seen a cartoon princess do when deep in thought, as I'd been told not to. I say: *My pet eats all the time.*

I sat in a chair. My mother knelt before me, carefully removing curlers, and brushed out my hair. She swept blush across my cheeks and twisted a pale green tube. The lipstick smelled thick and sweet, like solid lotion made of rose petals. I felt pretty and clean once I was ready. I sat patiently, as if onstage success depended on how I behaved during downtime.

She's not a baby but everyone calls her Baby Jane. She takes an audience request. Her sugary voice serenades a dead father. She kisses an envelope to stamp it, sends it skyward on a string rigged in the auditorium. The letter flails like a ghost above the audience.

We borrowed a pink lamé dress from a girl who was a winner. My mother covered plain ballet flats with shiny floral fabric. She made a flower from the remnants and sewed it onto a hair barrette. She pulled the plastic off the green couch. She styled my hair and makeup and I put on the outfit. I posed in the living room and she took pictures of me with my trophies. She mailed the developed photos to people who called themselves a modeling agency.

The pink and purple Conair hot sticks snapped my hair as they bent. I looked forward to the AquaNet clouds—chemical and floral smelling—fixing my hair in place, the feeling of being almost ready. I heard slight crunching when I moved my head. I liked folding over the cuffs on my ankle socks, fluffing the lace trim and feeling put-together.

She reprises her childhood act forty-five years later. She lives with and cares for her sister, whose fame eclipsed her own as they got older. She hires a pianist to come to their house. She makes her face up ghastly, styles her hair in bouncy curls. She wears Mary Janes and an adult-size replica of the white dress she wore as a girl.

A television show chronicles pageant contestants preparing to compete. Orange fog hisses spray tans. Airbrush pens mist faces yet to know blemishes. Impressions made of contestants' mouths; fake teeth, called flippers, cast to snap over imperfect smiles. I never knew these preparations.

The word *grotesque* sounds like an illness to me.

Watching the winner walk, smiling onstage, tears swelled in my stomach. It was Sweethearts or Winterfest. I slammed the car door, saying I did not win because I was ugly. The parking lot was full. I didn't want anyone to see me crying. I was too upset to stop.

*

I may have convinced myself winning was my destiny, or part of it. I may have missed a cue. In a photo from a crown ceremony where I received best attire and runner-up trophies, I smile at the trophy in each of my hands, instead of waving to the audience.

A girl in formalwear poses elaborately while the host describes her as an everyday girl. Taping the pageant, my father did not get the girl's mother in the frame. She stood at the back of the audience, doing the steps and gestures she wanted her daughter to repeat. The girl stands akimbo and tilts her head side to side, as if considering the audience and judges as they evaluate her.

The room looked like a shrunken hotel banquet hall—bland floor-length drapes, the carpet pattern like roses and sophisticated chain links, fan sconces cupping lights on the walls. I walked across the carpeting from one masking tape X to another, again and again. Each time, someone from the agency told me to do it different. Each time felt the same.

I was playing with my trophies and one fell, the winged woman with her arms to the sky in a victory pose. A chip flaked off, a shred of fake gold plating, revealing ugly brown plastic on one of the woman's wings.

In a makeshift dressing room—a closed store with pink carpeting and mirrored pillars—a girl squirmed on a chair near me. From the corner of my eye, I saw her mother's arm swing. I startled at the thunk—the hairbrush hitting the girl's head, plastic on bone. I sat exceptionally still.

*

Twice I flew to Texas to compete in a pageant for tattooed women. Preliminaries were held in Dallas, finals in San Antonio. Each event took place at a different tattoo convention and reflected traditional pageants. Hair and makeup artists dolled us up. A pageant director approved our wardrobe selections. We were asked to follow a code of conduct. One rule I recall clearly: *Don't get shit-face snockered in hotel rooms*, which I learned the director added after a contestant got drunk and someone photographed her nude in a hotel room. We were competing against each other, someone was judging us. We had something to live up to.

In an early 2000s remake of a '50s classic, six friends on a road trip encounter car trouble. They seek help in a small town with a noteworthy wax museum. The town is quaint and old fashioned: flyers advertise a beauty pageant for "Miss Ambrose," puppies wag their tails in a pet-store window, retro pumps outfit the gas station. The friends learn everything is wax—the homes, puppies, shops, and people. Even the nosy neighbor parting her curtains to gaze at the newcomers is guided by a motorized rig at the small of her back. The wax figures are rendered authentically lifelike because they were cast over the bodies of still-living people.

I ate lunch with another woman from the pageant. Over convention nachos and hot dogs, she complained about another contestant's attitude and the woman's mother, who hovered around the dressing room much of the weekend. All around, people got tattoos, bought jewelry and paintings. They paid to pose for photos with cult horror stars, like an actor from a Rob Zombie movie. We posed like pinup girls in our booth. Walking around the convention center, we stopped when people asked to photograph us. No one paid us for our pictures. In images the pageant photographer took of me, I could be a boardwalk caricature of myself—long fake lashes; mouth filled traffic-light red; hair teased full.

Two of the friends outrunning the murderous wax artist seek refuge in the movie theater. They sit among figures in different states of viewing—laughter, surprise, a hand reaching for popcorn—all the faces aglow. The reprise in *Whatever Happened to Baby Jane?* begins on screen, the grown woman in a girlish white dress sings sweetly—*I've written a letter to daddy, his address is Heaven above.*[1] [2]

*

I wanted to win too much for the lulls to feel boring. Each second tilted toward another chance to prove I was charming and beautiful. Sitting to preserve my hair and makeup seemed its own category because pageants included so much waiting—for my name read off an index card, my cue to walk onstage, to be seen, my feet to move from one tape X to the next, the breath of a question to end, the right rehearsed answer to exhale itself, for judges to decide I was pretty and poised. Advice and caution, curse and prayer, the phrase: *How you carry yourself.*

We practiced in the living room with the gold rug, the same place I rehearsed my walks and interviews. The everyday scenarios described in a slightly lower voice, the words slow and serious, made these moments sound dangerous: walk from a building to a car, cross a parking garage. My parents taught me to knee a man if he reached for me. They said to scream and run. They said to follow the script: *Stranger! I don't know this man!* They taught me to fill my mouth with my voice and flood the night with sound. My fist clutched my mother's car key between my index and middle fingers. My thumb pressed hard on the bow. I wanted to prove I could defend myself against bad people. The metal gleamed in my small fingers, sharp against my skin.

The girl who wore a royal-blue dress in the home movie moved in down the street. After school, we ate snacks and watched *Full House.* We pulled trophies from bedroom shelves. We asked our mothers to drag out photo albums of us all done up—poodle hair, bright powder streaking our cheekbones. Neither of us competed beyond the mall pageant circuit—January Winterfest, Starbursts, Sweethearts, Miss Camillus Mall. We were ten when the girl in Colorado died.

What happened to the girl in Colorado was not in my parents' lessons, depending on who you talk to and what they believe. The documentaries, *60 Minutes* specials, and *Lifetime* movie events they have seen. The newspapers, tabloids, blogs, or conspiracy theories they have read. The conversational wires crossing. The blank spaces awaiting new details to fill them.

At grocery store checkouts, I knotted with sadness and fear when I saw the Colorado girl's face on magazine covers. I didn't know why anyone would hurt her. Her face alongside magazines for cooking, travel, and fashion. The placement seemed shameful. Bold headlines leapt from tabloid covers. The story of a girl's life and death bought alongside the bread and eggs.

*

The roster of shopping malls that hosted pageants included Camillus, Penn Cann, Great Northern, and ShoppingTown. Each structure unique, with at least one glass revolving door, a food court, and a bright ceiling to marvel at while judges deliberated.

A mall is a collision of opportunities, a lifetime of starts and stops contained beneath one roof. Clothing retailers rotate signage with the seasons, jewelers sell engagement rings, furniture stores display cozy homescapes, wireless stores assure more bars, endless coverage, infinite connection. At the Arnot Mall in Horseheads, I once admired a tombstone store next to a sports chain called Finish Line, while eating a chocolate chip cookie with buttercream icing. The placement seemed like a well-imagined, mildly upsetting joke.

Plastic trophies awarded up the hall from a restaurant where lights hummed above all-you-can-eat salad bars. When I was old enough to go alone, I liked sifting through decor and accessories at Afterthoughts: neon candles shaped like peace signs, body glitter gel, nail polish, vinyl purses. I played SkeeBall at the arcade, traded in tickets for Jolly Ranchers. Meanwhile, a luxury ocean liner sank in staggered intervals across several Hoyts Cinemas screens. Neon tubes spelled the music store name on an awning, rows of jewel cases inside—Savage Garden, Backstreet Boys,

23

Spice Girls, No Doubt. I ate French fries in Burger King and read lyrics booklets while waiting for a parent's car to appear outside the entrance. The mall exhausted and excited me, everything happening at once.

*

The skeleton emerged from a former landfill, thickened across Onondaga Lake. Whenever my mother drove a stretch of I-690 beside the lake, she talked about an antique carousel restored to run inside the future mall.

A heavy wooden studio door swung shut on my foot after a dance class. Blood flowered under my big toenail, a spider-webbed crack. I waited for the nail to fall off.

The new mall opened, a mammoth white building with green edges and windows. My parents shepherded my siblings and me through the busy food court, toward the carousel. Someone stepped on my foot. Bandage fibers caught the crack in the nail and pulled it off. I sat on a wiry chair, felt the little squares press into the backs of my legs, embarrassed people saw my blood splashed against new pink tile. My mother wrapped my toe in Taco Bell napkins, tucked the edges under my sandal strap. I rode the carousel on a carriage with a maroon velvet seat. The view shifted from floor-to-ceiling windows to the food court; parking lot and lake beyond to Hooters, fast-food counters, an arcade. People watched from tables. Riders gazed from horse-back or carriages. Dizzy and spinning, all of us pulled along by bright carnival music.

Carousel rides became a frequent stop on mall visits. Waiting in line, I clutched a wooden admission token and studied the horses with floral garland necklaces, the detailed coaches. I liked the coach painted with a fancy-dressed woman on a swing. I wanted to be her, carefree and pretty, a pointy, kitten-heeled shoe dangled on her foot by a single toe.

Camillus Mall had mostly emptied by the late '90s and early aughts, save for abandoned display racks and stray hangers. Security grilles covered storefronts with dimmed signage, dry fountains flecked in coin sediment, green-white circles left by pennies tossed in the water to make wishes come true. Hoyts Cinemas and Bon-Ton were the last remaining businesses.

Friends and I went to the movies with some high school boys the weekend after eighth-grade graduation. One guy took a picture on a disposable camera, my friends and me smiling beneath an awning. The movie was long and loud. A woman in shorts and a black top braves ancient tombs with guns in thigh garters and a long, thick braid snaking down her back. One friend and I hung out in my neighbor's attic bedroom after the movie. She lifted the shirt she'd borrowed from me and flashed the guys. I lifted my shirt too, fast and nervous. I let my neighbor's cousin kiss me. He smelled of iced mint and sweat. His tongue tasted charred from smoking.

*

An atrium is a center, a heart, a view from which shoppers see stores, call across, wave.

*

Schoolchildren on a field trip to visit the Easter bunny stood in a line before a white gazebo in the atrium. The person in the Easter bunny costume ran to a neighboring Auntie Anne's pretzel cart for napkins and began cleaning. Barriers have not

25

been installed to prevent jumps and falls in the years since this incident, the first publicized suicide at Carousel Center in 1998.

The Carousel Center expansion, announced in the early 2000s, included a rebrand, a new name—Destiny USA. Additions include a comedy club, a hotel with a swimming pool, an indoor amusement park, glow golf, a Cheesecake Factory. Among the rotations, a Catholic chapel and religious gift shop took up residence on the mall's underground floor.

Destiny comes from the Latin verb *destinare*, meaning to make firm or establish. Destiny sounds like the inverse of doom to me, but the concept does not discern between luck, mediocrity, and misfortune, only the unseen certainty fate implies. *Destiny* is a more formal, elaborate-sounding word for endgame or future. The idea that some larger force verbs a life.

Glass elevators with soft-glowing number buttons rise and fall at the atrium's corners. I'd heard a rumor: non-employees could not ride elevators to the sixth floor because the top floors hosted offices, space for parties, weddings, and receptions. A friend and I took an elevator as high as we could. I don't remember whether we hit the fifth or sixth floor. We got out and didn't see anyone else. I looked over the rail, all the way down, my stomach dropped. The elevator had gone to another floor. While we waited for it to come back, I watched the thick cables moving the cars. Some hung slack. Others pulled taut to a complex system even higher overhead.

4.

This isn't a ghost story but I've become more aware of the furnace stopping, the sharp cutoff of air rushing into a room. In a homebuyer's class I listened to the instructor talk about heating systems. She preferred hot-water heat to forced air because even an annually serviced furnace carries dust of past dwellers through the ducts. The thought of someone else's sloughed skin gusting into her living space repulsed her. I think of decades blowing through the house.

I think of a haunted house movie. Characters take a tour, enter and leave rooms. They praise bathrooms, closets, kitchens, ballrooms. They lose each other and double back. They find secret passages. There's yearning in how they brush furniture and lift porcelain heirlooms from mantels, how they stare up at the ceilings and walls, take it all in.

The homebuyer's course met in a basement classroom of a building with historic designation, a former school. Lessons advised on how to save, track spending, improve credit scores. We were encouraged to forgo restaurant meals, coffee, shoes, and vacations in favor of homeownership, which assumed we all had money to spend on such luxuries. The instructor told us the word *mortgage*, broken down into its two parts, means death bond.

Disclosures in homebuying describe fine-print details about a house. They include property improvements, as well as warnings: lead paint, pests, property line disputes. Disclosure laws vary between states, so what a seller is legally obligated to note in California they may not be required to share in New York. The real estate phrase used to indicate a death—natural or otherwise—occurred on a property, or to admit a haunting, is *emotional defects*.

Visitors to the website diedinhouse.com type an address and pay a fee to learn who died there.

I pull up the cast iron register grates to vacuum out dust and pet hair. I find a small world in each, assorted items I collect atop a paper towel on the counter and drop into the trash: silica gel packets, two small plastic horses, pennies and nickels, a plastic floss pick.

*

Past lives push through on the air. How many people do I breathe in at my desk. How many ways may a house be a metaphor?

The reveal that feels truest to me in house horror, the one I most love: the dwellers have been haunting themselves all along.

*

A couple's car goes off a covered bridge, into a river. They return home and find their reflections lacking, a *Handbook for the Recently Deceased* on an end table. They are homebound or doomed to wander a desert of windstorms and sandworms. A new family moves in and redecorates.

The colonial in Scenic Hills was ripe for ghost stories. My brother told them. He convinced me the soffits hiding basement ductwork were an imaginary dead brother's coffin. The story I was told depended on my behavior, my brother's mood. A burglar murdered this brother and stuffed him in the box. A ghost buried him alive. Our parents put him there for not finishing his green beans. A tender, though still off-putting, version of this story: our brother died peacefully, asleep in his bed, and our parents buried him in the basement to keep him near the family.

My father stored tools and chemicals in the garage. Car oil and gasoline, pool treatments, seed packets, garden hose attachments, bottles of bright-hued liquids, stunningly toxic. Scanning the gray metal shelves, I may have imagined my insides shriveling, something hurting. I sat on the big green chest freezer, kicking my ankles against the enamel. I lay on the lid and heard a deep hum. I made snow angel arms and my hand on the back of the appliance felt the warmth it gave off from running. I lifted the lid to pick at sugar eggs my mother crafted one Easter, pastel dioramas with chocolate rabbits and chicks nested inside, green-tinted coconut pastures.

The daughter in the new family dresses in black and loves her camera. The father offers to build her a basement darkroom. The girl says: *My whole life is a darkroom. One big, dark room.* Her stepmother says, *Nonsense, you'll go to school, maybe meet a farm boy.*[1]

The professor for a poetry workshop I took noted how readily some people dismiss young people's feelings. She was not among them; she championed emotional honesty. Is the dismissal she described born of a belief in emotional scarcity, that only so much suffering exists in the world and everyone must jockey to win trophies for worst, saddest, most afraid? Is feeling a privilege unlocked at a particular age? An amusement park ride with a height chart staked at the entry. You must be X tall to feel Y. You must be A years old to feel B.

Or is the dismissal not of feeling but delivery, a disconnect between one person emoting and another person perceiving.

One spring, I visited a charter school to teach poetry classes. A few weeks into the sessions, a student sat with her head on her arms for the class period. Her teacher gently asked her to sit up and class carried on around the student, not without notice of her pain, but with no gesture of care, no remedy. Continuing the lesson seemed unfeeling, teaching poetry while someone expressed discomfort or pain.

Jenny Zhang explores emotional authenticity in her essay "How It Feels." She writes: *Darkness is acceptable and even attractive so long as there is a threshold that is not crossed.*[2]

I stood in the freezer with the lid opened. My brother held an uncapped bottle. Bright yellow sloshed inside. It looked magic to me, like lemons or sun, balloons or birthday-cake icing, sunflower petals or marshmallow Peeps. He told me to smell. I put my nose to the plastic lip, sniffed. I got so faint I nearly fell over. Another day I told my brother to bury me alive. I crouched among wire baskets, frozen vegetables, and frost. He closed the lid.

*

The couple visits afterlife social services to complain about the new family. Death is as everyday as errands and work. Decedents sit in a cramped waiting room. They hold long Take-A-Number slips and await caseworkers. The wife asks her husband: *Is this what happens when you die?*

The receptionist, a beauty pageant contestant with wrist wounds, says: *This is what happens when you die. That is what happens when he dies. And that is what happens when they die. It's all very personal. And I'll tell you something. If I knew then what I know now, I wouldn't have had my little accident.*[3]

The last owners of the house in Scenic Hills were tragic, accord-
ing to my brother. The husband was unfaithful to his wife, so she murdered him and buried him in the bathroom, the shower wall white with beige tiles in the corners and center. I imagined the man eternally sprawled in the architecture while I bathed, the beige tiles his decomposing hands, feet, and head.

I put my head underwater and listened. I felt included but sepa-
rate, like a ghost eavesdropping on house and dwellers, what they want, how they shout and creak. I waited for my ears to fill with water and believed my whole self could too. This was before the babysitting course where I learned a person can drown in what seems a negligible depth of water. I practiced swaddle techniques and compressions on a plastic baby with a rubber chest that gave beneath my hands when I pressed. We learned how dangerous a house can be, all the stairs, corners, and outlets.

*

A neighborhood may be a helix of lookalikes, details borrowed for practicality or aesthetic, repeated for continuity. I feel a con-
nected tug when I notice duplicates on adjacent streets, or one detail reflecting another in a different city. An aluminum awning in Ithaca like my grandparents' Pittsburgh patio. An ornate porch

rail calls to mind iron lace scrawled across the balcony on a pastel New Orleans home. Purple and teal slate tiles, the path to the front door of the Scenic Hills house. Porch pillars like those towering on Syracuse University's fraternity and sorority row.

Picnic tables, benches, and people crowd the patio. A line snakes from a sliding window. We consider options out loud like distracted prayer: soft-serve twist or vanilla, sprinkles or not. The menu board is white with red and blue writing, like the menu from a Syracuse ice cream shop popular after dance recitals or soccer games. Convertible tights rolled to knees, grass-stained jerseys shimmered in sun, jelly sandals and cleats clicked on pavement. The smell of frozen cream and sugar softened the large white house behind us, its funeral parlor sign. It's a weird coincidence the Ithaca ice cream shop is across from two churches. People in suits on the steps could be waiting for a wedding or a funeral. I look for a limo or hearse.

That even cremains are often buried and cemeteries gated, some contained by tall, thick walls of stone, distinctly separates life and death. One or the other, either/or.

I had a dog who choked himself on walks, huffed and pulled on the leash along a cemetery fence. I ran through another cemetery visiting my father in Wisconsin. Partway through, tightness wrung my chest and spit filled my mouth. I walked back to the gates. It was different than Syracuse, the cemetery I passed as I ran on a sidewalk. Knee-high posts and chain divided me from the dead. In the street, yellow lines divided oncoming and opposing traffic, separated drivers from collision, injury, their own possible deaths.

I type in our address at diedinhouse.com. Besides deaths in my house, the site sells additional reports: past fires, whether my home was ever a meth lab, where the nearest sex offenders live, as well as practical details, like past sales and tax assessments. Our house is thirteen years shy of one hundred. It's easy to assume someone died here. The question is how. Was the death natural or not, violent or peaceful, unexpected? Do I want to know?

The disturbances in *Poltergeist* are fun at first. The mother outfits her youngest daughter in a football helmet. She sets her in a hand-drawn circle on the kitchen floor and delights as an invisible force pulls the girl to another circle across the room. The spirit presence is intriguing until the girl gets sucked into their realm. Meanwhile, earth-moving machines decorate the family's backyard, digging up the dirt to install a swimming pool. Only the developer knows all the sweet houses in Cuesta Verde were built atop anonymous bodies. The development company moved the headstones—but not the bodies—and the souls are understandably angry.

A bone found beneath a garden may be undeniably animal, but was the animal wild or a pet? Who buried the animal? Did someone pray after they tamped the dirt?

I don't buy the diedinhouse.com report. I tell myself I don't want to pay for the information. The truth is I'm too afraid to know.

*

Driving to the Outer Banks, Dave and I crossed the Chesapeake Bay Bridge Tunnel. Twenty-three miles with two mile-long tunnels in the middle to let boats cross above. Each time the car entered an underwater tunnel, I held my breath. I closed my eyes until I guessed we were almost out. I thought of the tunnels collapsing, how fast it would happen. Whether we'd have time to feel fear. I waited to see the light that seemed to pull us back above ground and water.

A grade-school friend and I shared an interest in the paranormal and urban legends. We checked out school library books on Bigfoot, the Loch Ness Monster, UFO sightings. Light often appeared in the encounters. A man driving his motorcycle on a dark road nearly hit a creature with a long, thin neck and round body seen by moonlight. Or a beam of light shot from a heap of night clouds. I asked my friend, *Do you think it's all real?* He said, *I've got to believe.*

One spring, a classroom where I taught at dusk became an illuminated fish tank fifteen minutes into class. People outside could see us. I felt uneasy I could not see them back. The room felt separate from everything outside it. The fall had felt different. I'd walked from the building and seen sunsets, days ending. On campus one evening, I sat in my office after class and watched the sun burn the treetops and hills with pink-gold light. Looking warmed me, light blushing the office, folding the small room and me into the landscape. In the spring, we went toward the light with each class.

Light is comfort and relief, familiar and known. On a Thursday, a pinhole of the coming weekend punctures the monotony. Or a project is almost complete and, *There's a light at the end of the tunnel.*

The family connects with the daughter in the other realm. The girl sees a bright light. Her mother says, *Stay away from the light. The light is dangerous. Don't go near it. Don't even look at the light.*[4]

A common trope about dying is we see a bright light as we fade. We walk toward the light to die. We walk into the light. Maybe it's religious: we meet a god, we're reunited with people who died before us. It's reassuring: we're going toward the light, it's not so bad.

Funeral director Thomas Lynch says: *A good funeral is one that gets the dead where they need to go and the living where they need to be.*[5]

The family hires a medium who explains: *There is no death. There is only a transition to a different sphere of consciousness. Carol Anne is not like those she's with. She's a living presence in their spiritual, earth-bound plane. They're attracted to the one thing about her that's different from themselves. Her life-force—it is very strong. It gives off its own illumination.*[6]

The State Theatre shows *Poltergeist.* During some scenes everyone laughs like we're all in on the same inside joke. Or everyone becomes very quiet. The medium's speech calls to mind children haunted and haunting, connecting one side of life to the other.

On screen, I wear a blue shirt with a gold wildcat printed on the front. The cotton hangs to my knees, the sleeves wide around my arms. Outside the frame, my mother holds the camcorder on her shoulder, taping my message: *Billina's in there and Tik-Tok and Dorothy.* I point at the lens where I think movie characters live. I break the fourth wall. Lens black reflecting a blue shine.

Viewers watch a videotape and a phone rings. A raspy voice gives the viewer a week to live. A ghost girl haunts her audience.

Dreary weather, a blue-gray patina shading faces. Details from the tape begin appearing in the characters' daily lives like morbid tarot figures—a fly, a ladder, a split nail, a frightened horse, a team of drowning horses, a millipede. A boy sees the tape and soon after communicates with the ghost girl. He tells his mother: *She lives in a dark place now.*[7]

Some feelings are clearer to me than stories I've been told. Lying in my dark bedroom, the green coverlet with thin vertical lines running the length. The curtains drawn. Street-and-snow light pressed through, carved a purple square in the wall. Awash in a largeness, a calming wave before I felt the plunge. An enormous hand picking me up, hurling me toward a vast feeling.

*

The basement in the first apartment we rented in Ithaca was creepy. I accessed it through a door outside the house, which was often left unlocked. The ceiling was low. Stringy webs draped from overhead pipes. The wall above the laundry machines had a gaping hole that opened into blackness, a room under the studio apartment behind ours.

Hands on a leather cover, a dagger blade opens uncut pages. A woman's voice reads from an antique book that claims three evil sister spirits haunt and rule the earth. A sketch on the wall of the woman's apartment building resembles an illustration in the book, the home to Mater Tenebrarum, the Mother of Darkness.

Stagnant water filled the washer. Dave reached into the water and found no clothes in the drum. Our landlord called a handyman, a plumber, and then the city. The problem exceeded the appliance. Hair-thin tree roots had grown through the pipes, feeding on the waste and water being carried from the house.

The roots had backed water up into the washer as they thrived, thick as the thumbs of the men who came to cut up the sidewalk. One of them showed me. I asked what was happening. He held up his thumb for reference.

The woman wanders the old apartment building's basement like a cave system, diagonal beams and cobwebs. She follows a stream in the floor to a pool of water. She stoops to look and her keys slip from her wrist. The keychain is a warning, if the rhyme for identifying snakes holds true: *Red touches black, safe for Jack. Red touches yellow, kill a fellow.* Red and black beads separated by gold bands indicate a coral snake. She gets in the water to retrieve her keys. It's deeper than it looks, a gothic-furnished underwater apartment, hazy and blue. A watery otherworld of amplified creaks and plunks, drenched furniture and decorations. Dreamy until a decomposing corpse floats by her.

Dave and I followed the door off the laundry room to the rest of the basement. It felt like the moment in a horror movie when something moves in the dark and it's a raccoon, bird, or bat. The moment opens into another; the characters laugh so hard at themselves for being afraid, they miss the shadow approaching them. I was relieved to find the fuse box in a middle room, not the furthest back, the dark room behind the laundry machines. Chalky dust smell. The old water tank's tart metal snap. The earthy wafts of being even slightly below ground. A plastic clamshell sat on a ledge, new fuses to fit on the board. Old, blown fuses scattered on the floor.

5.

We sat in a sculpture court between two campus buildings. Ivan Meštrović's bronze *Job* looked miserably up at the sky. *Supplicant Persephone* stood in a posture of surrender and plead—face turned skyward, arms stretched up, one leg slightly bent. I was used to the idea of us breaking up until it happened. It shifted from a worry to something real and we both cried sitting on the stone bench. He kept his sunglasses over his eyes. I felt heavy and breathless at once, so overwhelmed by sadness I couldn't help crying on the bus to my apartment. I ordered sushi delivery, cried and ate, watching TV in my room on my laptop. When I took my dishes downstairs, my face was pink and swollen. My roommate had a friend visiting, a psychology major who spoke in the loud way that addresses someone without speaking directly to them: *Adults crying is their way of having a temper tantrum. It's saying, "I don't have what I want, give me what I want."*

Bat silhouettes flutter across the fabric and white letters drip down the black top: *America's Most Haunted*. I put on Lana Del Rey and bake. I think of her watery music videos, dreamy hues paired with dark lyric currents, how admitting sadness, devotion, love, desire, and fear is a kind of strength: *No one compares to you/I'm scared that you/Won't be waiting on the other side.*[1]

I pipe French macarons, crimp piecrusts, spoon cookie dough onto parchment paper. By the time I carry what I make to the party, I'll be wearing something else, a sunflower-and-daisy-print skirt, a coral blouse with a sweet collar. I won't be in the frame of the photo I snap to post the dessert on the Internet. On the speakers, an ethereal, ghostly *Oh* trails off like an afterthought.

It's inadvisable to embrace a low feeling, to wallow. I don't know how to say I'm sad without thinking I sound childish. I've heard interior darkness described as precious, goth, morbid, intense. It's not polite conversation. It's a punchline or parody, an archetype, an act, a cry for help. It's en vogue to admit a feeling or claim acceptance of it—in oneself or others; it's hard to genuinely accept it. It's *a conversation we need to have* that seems impossible to broach without bringing down a mood or inciting concern. Admitting a feeling is not the same as seeking a solution; sometimes saying *I feel X* is the solution.

Darkness may unfold slowly at first and gain momentum, like a time-lapse film showing a plant growing or the sun setting. As in Denis Johnson's poem "Now": *And so does my life tremble, / and when I turn from the window / and from the sea's grief, the room / fills with a dark / lushness and foliage nobody / will ever be plucked from, / and the feelings I have / must never be given speech.*[2]

A steady fall builds intensity. A push-and-pull impulse—want versus hesitation to name the feeling, to sit patiently with darkness and study it: line or liquid, expanding breath. How does light cut through and refract? What does the light hit? Does it bounce back or keep going?

*

A passage collapse traps six friends in a cave system's dark, narrow tunnels. One woman admits she has led her friends to an unknown system, instead of the mapped one they planned to visit. The women go deeper into the cave in search of another exit. One or two miles underground, they encounter a gorge that seems vertically infinite. Maneuvering a Tyrolean traverse, the women find dated climbing equipment lodged in the rock, a long-ago explorer's attempt to cross. Proof someone else was there, but not that they made it out.

I try to stop the feeling—rather than slow my descent. I feel more upset. I tell myself, *This is just a feeling.* I shrink the intensity. I telescope heaviness with words like *only* and *just.*

From one of Paul Celan's "Microliths": *The poem's hour of birth... lies in darkness. Some claim to know that it is the darkness just before dawn; I do not share this assumption.*[3]

No one needs the promise of a sunrise to create. Daylight can throw reality into a relief bleaker than the dark, unseen, and unknown.

Gorges and tunnels extend beyond what's expected. In a cavern, led by headlamps and a video recorder's night vision, the women scan the cave floor strewn with bones, illuminated soft and green—*Dead animals! Hundreds of them!*[4] Someone flicks a lighter to find a breeze. The recorder's gaze shifts. One woman stands still, green and stunned. Beyond her shoulder, a humanoid creature looms before diving for the ground and crawling up the wall to the ceiling.

Who decided despair was darkness? Who feels it as an awful painful blast of light?

*

The Witley Park estate in Surrey includes the underwater ballroom of James Whitaker Wright, a criminal businessman who took his life after being sentenced. In the estate's man-made lake, a statue of the sea god Neptune appears to float. The statue is set atop a domed aquarium. At night, a soft green glow brightens the water beneath Neptune's feet, as if he walks on yellow-green, algae-tinted light. A door on land opens to a spiral staircase descending beneath the lake. The staircase opens to tunnels curving to the secret room—a smoking lounge, ballroom, and parlor.

I am among those who fear submerged objects. Those things intended to float that failed—shipwrecks—and those that don't belong underwater at all—defunct subway cars sunk to build an artificial reef.

I think of the movie with a con preacher who murders his wife and drives her car into a lake with her tied in the passenger seat. Underwater, her hair dances like the seaweed floating around her.

A recent neo-noir film traces the decline of a mostly abandoned city called Lost River. To lift the curse hovering over the city someone must retrieve an item from the bottom of the lake— a town flooded during a reservoir's construction. The town's streetlights still click on at darkfall, the posts half submerged. A boy goes into the water at night. Seeing him break the murky surface and swim down I want to know how long he can hold his breath. What else is alive in the water? How do the lights still come on?

How true is it that bringing something from the past to the surface will break the curse?

Sitting inside in winter, windows frosted over, a world happening outside. My dark place is not characterized by lack of light, but submersion. Like soaking in a bathtub, putting my head under and hearing words I can't unravel; muffled, metallic ringing through enamel; the architecture's internal creaks, wood groaning small adjustments, expanding or contracting, the overflow plate gulping water. I hold my breath and count how long the house is quiet. My dark place feels like being immersed in a plunge pool while a waterfall rages overhead, a surge so intense it seems to morph from liquid to solid. The current may submerge a person and turn them into a body. The body can get pushed so far down the search requires deep-sea divers. My dark place feels like being carried by a creek, ebbing on to empty into something larger.

6.

In satin pajamas and high heels, a young woman runs out of her house into a peaceful street at dusk. A neighbor asks if she's okay. The young woman stares at a fixed point and backs up slowly. Her father stands concerned in the yard. She runs inside for her car keys and speeds off. She sits on a beach. The car's headlights shine like a spotlight on her. The water behind her dark with sparkling flecks. The night sky and darkness at the frame edges like the borders of a tintype photograph. She's on her phone with her parents, apologizing and saying she loves them. She stares at her car, the driver door flung open. Then it's morning and she's dead, one leg bent back and broken, blood running down the thigh. The water and sky behind her a crisp-perfect blue, horrific and serene. One could almost imagine a boat with a bright sail out on the water.

Two friends, my husband, and I sit in the second tier. Panic looms and dips from my chest at the jolt of periodic jump scares. A pulsing synth soundtrack buzzes in my teeth and toes.

A college student has sex with her new boyfriend. A fatal, slow-walking, persona-shifting specter begins to follow her. Like a dreadful parlor game, a person being followed must have sex with someone else to survive. That partner must pass "It" along in the same way.

I re-watch the movie and among the brick houses and schools, green lawn-checkered suburbs, blue swimming pools, the soft-lit all-night diner, parking lots and sidewalks, I catch a slow-walking form I missed before and I feel I have missed something larger. Perhaps I am ascribing significance to something that does not deserve any. This same flawed hindsight informs my assumption I could have known people in my life were planning their deaths.

It's hard not to think the film trains me to look for these figures. Once I start seeing them, I notice more omens. I search for them. The *Ithaca is gorges* tee shirts and bumper stickers. Coffee mugs in green, red, and navy: *Ten square miles surrounded by reality.*

Each image vivid and crisp. The dreamy and realistic juggled, the abstraction of anxious thoughts solidified into image. Much of what fills the frame is an almost-real beautiful nightmare, a visualization of a feeling that falls between fearful gallop and always-ache.

The feeling is as everyday as the third step on the staircase creaking and cars on the street, part of the scenery. The marquee ticker tape in my head I've been encouraged to acknowledge and watch float past. An exercise wheel where a rodent runs so fast it tips the apparatus as I try to calm the animal to a casual mall-walk.

Her boyfriend rummages in the trunk. She lies across the seat in her underwear, stretches an arm out the open door. Her hand brushes flowering weeds sprouted from concrete in the lot and she says: *I used to daydream about being old enough to go on dates... I had this image of myself holding hands with a really cute guy, listening to the radio, driving along some pretty road up north maybe, when the trees started to change colors. It was never about going anywhere really... just having some sort of freedom, I guess.*[1]

My dread has no origin. It extends back as far as I remember. Sometimes I don't know if I'm sick or anxious—fatigue sends me to bed for days, nausea, a scratchy throat, headaches, fevers. Does anxiety lower my immunity and make me sick, or do I shut down when I'm excessively anxious? What comes first and does it matter? It's chicken and egg and both are real.

Her boyfriend drugs her with chloroform. She comes to in a parking garage, tied to a wheelchair. Her boyfriend explains: *This thing, it's gonna follow you.*[2]

Something followed me when I was a girl. I don't know what it was; spirit, monster, or shadow. My parents woke at night to me cry-screaming. They'd rush into my room and find me sitting up, staring into the dark. I'd put a finger to my mouth and say, *Shh, the Four-Day Win.* I remember being in that bedroom, my parents flustered in the doorway. I don't remember what I'd seen.

The Four-Day Win may have been a mondegreen, a phrase I misheard and repeated, a mistaken object name. Part of me believes it was something I felt, a phrase for a heavy feeling. My mother checked my room for a draft, something making me uncomfortable. She looked for an explanation, a source beyond my saying.

*

I used to perch on the bathroom sink, the full-length mirror on the door facing the cabinet mirror. I moved the door on its hinges, slightly opening and closing it, doing the same with the cabinet, to make an infinity—a space that went back and back into more mirrors, more me's. I wondered how far back the mirrors could go before there was no more me at all.

At night when I looked out my bedroom window and saw the sky I thought of space, the universe going on. I felt the planet pulse around me. Was that distance the same as my mirror infinity: space stretched out, silence doing the same. Like heavy snowfall devours streets and driveways, mutes the world. Snow's ambient noise impedes sound waves and accumulates quiet. Even silence is a sound wave following us.

When it's snowing, the outdoors seem like a room, writes David Berman in his poem "Snow." *Today I traded hellos with my neighbor./Our voices hung close in the new acoustics./A room with the walls blasted to shreds and falling.*[3]

People on the sidewalk, or in line at the grocery store, bank, post office. People at the park with dogs or babies. Maybe we're all looking out for "It." Days filled as postponement or temporary escape from what walks slowly toward us.

She and her friends hide at a lake house. They rig windows and doors with traps to signal an intruder. They relax on the beach. She sits alert in a chair, staring at the water. Her friend walks toward the beach on a path behind her and a cut shows the same friend in the water, splashing by on a floaty, asking who else wants to swim.

Company doesn't immunize me to dread. I take too long to decide on a comfortable and flattering outfit to wear to a party. Once I'm there, I can't settle on a room, who to talk to, getting a drink or food. I find a seat or corner and stay there as long as possible. Throughout the night, my voice changes. An exuberant, higher tone at first that drops. As I become comfortable, my laugh comes from my stomach instead of wispy exhales from my throat. Still, sometimes I feel the room shrinking, the air temperature escalating and I suddenly want to leave, an invisible large-looming force the puppeteer to this feeling.

On the beach, her hair is pulled to stand on end. Something her friends can't see drags her from her seat. "It" appears to her as her friend who spends the film reading Dostoevsky's *The Idiot* on a clamshell device, reciting lines like: *I think that if one is faced by inevitable destruction—if a house is falling upon you, for instance—one must feel a great longing to sit down, close one's eyes and wait, come what may.*[4] [5]

Or as the poet Frank Stanford writes in "The Nocturnal Ships of the Past": *There was always a great darkness/moving out/like a forest of arrows*[6]

Horror derives from Latin, *horrere*—to bristle with fear, shudder—which became the French *horreur*—a feeling of disgust—and later, emotion of horror or dread. It's the repulsion that comes after terror, anxious anticipation. Horror is a reaction, recognition, a response to a call.

She echoed past midnight from a space larger than the living room. My living room door was opened to the front hall. My cat was meowing and climbing the stairs to the second floor. The outside door was unlocked but closed. I locked it, brought in my cat, locked the living room door. I worried we'd narrowly missed something terrible. I opened my laptop, put on the '70s-set music-tour-and-coming-of-age movie. I told myself I'd been sleepwalking.

I got out of the shower another night to a missed call. I assumed a wrong number, a telemarketer, but the local number was familiar. Sitting on my bed in my pink towel, past phone bills confirmed the number belonged to someone I'd told not to call me anymore. Someone I feared.

Does knowing come before the body's reaction? Does the body know before the mind? Was all this already there? Is my circuitry a template for fear or a result of being alive?

*

Can a chainsaw be a god? A masked person's bare hands? Rage laid bare. A blade turned back on a killer. The call from inside the house star-sixty-nined before it's too late.

Ancient theatergoers delighted as a crane lowered a savior to a set, or a hero rose from beneath a trapdoor in the stage. Deus ex machina endorses the possibility of rescue from the terminal cusp, salvation in a moment of ultimate despair and hopelessness.

Some possible thing flickers in the dark. Walking alone at night, I hear a sound besides my own feet. Someone else's footsteps or an animal. A screen door whines open, a car door slams shut. It seems right a sudden onset of fear is compared to a wave; it shatters the idea that I am alone and breaks on me like an egg in a slumber-party song meant to augur death or some other enormous misfortune. *Crack an egg on your head, let the yolk run down.*

Door dead-bolted, windows locked shut, curtains flung back. My heartbeat can be the most horrifying sound in a room if I can't slow the organ's rhythm.

The word *anxious* was preceded by the Latin *anxius*—troubled in mind—born from *angere*—to choke, like something stuck in the throat, obscuring oxygen's path to the lungs, or breath held in response, fighting or flying, a deep inhale before a dive.

7

Half of us wore white, half wore black. Cotton leotards with sheer skirts attached. The teacher gathered us in a circle. She gave one girl a small bottle. Each of us dabbed a dot of tangerine oil on our palms and feet. A sweet citrus tang swirled the rehearsal room beneath the stage. We held hands with the people beside us. We whispered *Merde* for good luck.

Backstage, a butterfly horde rose through me. Wings bottlenecked in my chest. Other words describe nervousness: jitters, heebie-jeebies, screaming meemies, the willies. The latter is said to evoke physical discomfort, a late-nineteenth-century word *probably in reference to the itchiness of wool garments.*

The willies could also descend from *Giselle*, a ballet in which a peasant girl learns her beloved deceived her and she takes her life. The Wilis summon Giselle to rise from her grave. They wear bridal-white costumes, sometimes veils. The dancers appear to float across the stage.

The Wilis are affianced maidens who have died before their wedding-day, according to Heinrich Heine, the writer whose description of these ghosts inspired the libretto to *Giselle. In their hearts which have ceased to throb, in their dead feet, there still remains that passion for dancing which they could not satisfy during life; and at midnight they rise up and gather in bands on the highway and woe betide the young man who meets them, for he must dance until he drops dead.*[1]

Giselle is not an anomaly in ballet canon. Heartbreak, dark magic, death, and ghosts frequent story ballets. In *La Sylphide*, a man abandons his bride on their wedding day to pursue a spirit love who dies. In *Swan Lake*, a sorcerer turns a woman to a swan and tricks the swan-woman's lover into betraying her. *Romeo and Juliet* ends like its dramatic ancestor, with two lovelorn teenagers ending their lives.

I changed from my school clothes in a dim bathroom stall. Organ music played in a chapel up the hall. I put up my hair, slid a pilled zip-up over my shoulders. My slippers whispered down the carpeted stairs to the church basement. Some afternoons, I arrived before anyone else. The lights weren't on yet. The room outside the studio glowed red-dark from the EXIT sign.

*

I liked the preparations, the small tasks and routines. Stretch before class, barre before floor. Stitch elastics and ribbons to pointe shoes. Cut the ribbon on a diagonal, sweep a lighter flame along the edge to prevent fray.

Sounds other than music occurred to me on a frequency of the body. I can still hear as much as feel: pink slippers hushing across a studio floor, water sloshing in my stomach, my left ankle cracking as I circle the foot, a rosin rock breaking beneath a satin shoe in a pine box.

The coven running the ballet academy in *Suspiria* protects the founder, the Mother of Sighs. In one scene, a dancer outruns a mysterious person pursuing her through the ballet school. She enters a room filled with razor wire. Blue light, her body tangled. Her anguished cries split open the night.

Like nervousness, pain is a reply to stimuli. Suffering or distress responding to X.

I assumed injuries happened dramatically, not quietly, in stretch class, folded nose to knees: ache like a wide sash tying itself across my lower back.

Any movement the dancer in the wire makes to escape worsens her pain. She crawls and reaches for the door standing slightly ajar. She gets more caught in the wire coils.

I wanted the work to appear feather-light. I tried to be a line. I sucked in, envisioned a horizontal string inside me, tying navel to spine. I wilted without slouching when an instructor said, *I can see your lunch.* I saw myself swell in the mirror, imagined a sandwich outline and peach slice silhouettes pressing through my leotard.

Another instructor's jaw fell long when she said *Cow*, as if saying the small word was as painful as hearing it. I kept my head in place, dropped my eyes to her feet. Her peach-pink teacher shoes with short, square heels reminded me of pig hooves.

*

A dance friend's mother took us swimming at a motel pool. Orbs on the pool walls lit the water, cool and clear, the bottom scratchy with sand. My lungs tightened from treading too long, kicking my legs wide beneath the water, waving my arms in port de bras at the surface. My friend and I tracked cat litter from the garage through her house, up to her room. We stood in damp swimsuits and tee shirts before her bedroom TV. My friend clicked the remote. She stopped on a man kissing a woman and telling her to kiss another woman. The man put his hands under a skirt, someone sighed. I kept looking. My friend called me weird, or she called the movie weird, and changed the channel. I felt embarrassed. Litter between my toes scratched on the rug.

It's Latin for *breathlessness, sighs. Suspiria.* The word, a whisper, something felt as it's heard. Two hushed heartbeat pulses.

*

I fastened a butterfly clip in my hair and slipped my feet in the pink canvas shoes. Kneeling chair to chair, I studied the costumes in photos on the wood-paneled walls. Tulle and nylon, elastic and ribbon; textiles that give and those that resist. The studio director came in and we talked about the company. She described success as *sweating blood.* She said it with the familiarity and fondness someone might invoke telling a nostalgic anecdote that ends, *It was fine.*

Merde means *shit* in French. Mythology shrouds why some dancers say it before they perform. I've heard *Break a leg* is unlucky. Performances used to include live animals and *Merde* was a warning to watch one's step onstage. When horse-and-carriage was prime transport, messy streets meant many horses had carried many people to the theater, a full audience.

*

I stretched on the floor in my black leotard and skirt. Musicians overhead took their seats. Stands and chair legs scraped the stage. The dance ensemble waited our turn. I felt like a cellist who opened her case to find a violin resting in the ruby velvet.

A scene in *Suspiria*'s 2018 reimagining shows a new dancer rehearsing after another dancer quits. The veteran dancer wanders the massive academy, distraught. She finds a secret studio, the walls made entirely of mirrors, the room looks prismatic. Both dancers perform. They move as if beguiled by an unseen force. The new dancer exhilarated; the trapped dancer tormented, her movements violent, painful echoes of the new dancer's. Her face contorts. She twists and bends until her bones break. The new dancer's rising star agonizes the veteran dancer's departure.

Some sentiments invite good luck and others ward off bad luck. A distinction lies between wishing for success and deflecting misfortune.

During a private rehearsal, the company's creative director tells the new dancer: *When you dance the dance of another you make yourself in the image of its creator. You empty yourself so that her work can live within you.*[2]

A ritual is *performed according to set sequence*. The body knows rituals: respiration, digestion, circulation, sleep-wake, dream. The body exists within a cycle. The body is a finite cycle.

Our number blended ballet and modern dance. The choreography and costumes portrayed us as the light and the dark, not as good and evil, the instructor had said, but balance. I was night. I smelled like tangerine.

*

The tattoo artist changed his gloves after he completed each step. He cautioned, *It will stretch out when you have kids.* I said I didn't want any. He said, *Every girl says that.* We each sounded sure. I might have felt less defensive had he said *if you have kids*; had he issued equal caution about sun exposure. Stickers edged his station mirror. I read: *Pain is weakness leaving the body.* He washed my skin and wiped it dry, pressed the transfer paper flat. A violet stencil stained my skin.

*

I pay five dollars to browse the New Orleans Pharmacy Museum. Displays show remedies, analgesics, herbs, photos, and tools. I look for leeches and find none. I see a box for tampons steeped in opium, belladonna, and hyoscyamus to ease headaches, cramping, and dysphoria. Upstairs, a birthing chair, forceps, an exam table with extended stirrups. The instruments inspire body horror, an unease they have been used. Looking at speculums in neat rows on a shelf, duck-mouths faced the same way, I hear the metal clicking sound they make when opened.

*

Small lightning jolted inside me. I stayed up scrolling online forums, nervous the device would not work if it had shifted. The next morning a nurse removed mine, partially expelled after a year and a half. *The Cadillac of birth control* I'd read or heard, which seemed strange when I saw it on a tray: plastic and copper, two trailing hair-fine filaments. I wanted to wrap it in paper towels and stuff it in my purse. I wanted another, even though I knew it could happen again.

A babysitter takes a job the night of a monumental lunar eclipse. She moves around the old house, through ornate rooms, settling in a television den. A news anchor explains the eclipse is *well underway... The best time to see this fascinating event will be just about the stroke of midnight. That's when you'll be able to see the moon itself disappear into the Earth's shadow.*[3]

I swallowed some Valium and ibuprofen and walked to my doctor's office. A man in the hall outside my exam room sat with his arm cuffed, a machine measuring his blood pressure. The nurse and I talked about her children and kombucha. She measured my depth and I made a feral sound. I worried the man was still in the hall. I felt embarrassed he had heard me. The lights above the exam table winced back at me.

The babysitter orders a pizza, which she notes tastes off as she eats. She wavers dizzy when the moon passes into the Earth's shadow. She wakes in throbbing light, dressed in a white frock, tied to a pentagram. She is at the center of some ritual. People gather around her. They trace bloody symbols on her skin. She escapes and runs upstairs. A woman from the ritual finds her and says: *No matter what you do, it won't stop. It can't be stopped. You'll see. It's going to work in spite of you.*[4] The two women struggle, blood smeared on them both.

Tools gleamed silver-sterile, a long swab smeared in iodine, a torn-open package, a rust-colored streak on paper. The nurse said, *Women have been putting things up there forever to not get pregnant.* I felt calm, reassured, *This will work.* My *No* was not unique or permanent. I was joining a long line of refusal or postponement; one more person making a choice in the lineage.

*

Thinking of my biological clock is different from being reminded I have one. Familiar refrains take on unnerving tones as they accumulate. Like a baby magicked to life by rhyme-logic: *First comes love, then comes marriage, then comes X with a baby carriage.* The verse omits longing and assumes everyone in love gets married, everyone married moves from love to baby with ease, if they do so at all.

A woman wearing red pajamas floats on a mattress in crisp water. She descends a staircase and lies down on a bed. A creature climbs atop her. *The dreams I had,* she says the next morning, bright scratches on her back. The husband says, *I didn't want to miss the night,* rather than confirm her suspicion: *I think it was someone inhuman.*[5] Dread resides within her, radiates pain's red flag. Softness does not save her. Wide-eyed innocence, a tendency to talk with a finger near her mouth. Tenderness renders her susceptible to condescension. Other characters assure her everyone knows what's best for her and her unborn child, except her.

I want to understand the impulse to tell someone a secret about their life, whether or not the secret is true. Someone said: *Eventually you'll hit an age when you won't be able to stop it. You'll think, "I need a baby."* I found this creepy. The rigid certainty; want as something that would happen to me, instead of a way I might someday feel.

*

Maybe, but probably not doesn't sound like an answer, even though it is. I exaggerate not wanting. On Mother's Day, my husband and I bury our faces in our hands as a man transforms into a fly on the TV. His pregnant girlfriend has a nightmare about giving birth to an infant-size maggot. It writhes from her. Doctors grasp for it. Who am I trying to convince with my performance of disgust? What am I grasping for?

I crawled into bed with a heating pad and stared at the window. Silhouettes blurred the curtains. Voices floated cloaks and witch hats toward a Halloween festival.

A woman's son imitates a videotape magician: *Nothing in my hands. Nothing in my hands. Life is not always as it seems. It can be a wondrous thing, but it can also be very treacherous.*[6]

The woman's husband died driving her to the hospital to give birth. She and her son live swathed in grief. Gloom swallows their home in sorrow-damp, blue-gray hues. A monster manifests from a book the son reads about a shadow in a tall top hat that offers increasingly threatening verses: *I'll soon take off my funny disguise./Take heed of what you've read./Once you see what's underneath,/you're going to wish you were dead.*[7]

Any thought I share feels like an idea I must live up to forever. Still, I sometimes imagine reading in a nursery, my arms warm and heavy. A movie-perfect moment; unmined ore, raw footage; a nice thought not calcified into want, untouched by time and social pressure.

The mother's grief-rage and the shadow expand alongside the son's obsession with the monster, even though the mother swears it is not real.

One person's certainty can stretch like a shadow over someone else's want. I've heard if I wait until I'm ready I will never be ready. I hear I have time. I hear *The heart cracks open*; the phrase is a challenge and a selling point. Advice overlaps. Shadows swallow each other. They offer shade. They can obscure the frightening just as easily as they can veil the beautiful. Depending on time and light, the shadows' edges change, their intensity dims or deepens.

*

People wearing expensive blue suits tie me to my bed in a nightmare. They say, *We have to take it.* I wake convinced they meant the plastic braced inside me, but what if they meant a baby? I may keep having this dream, unsure what they want. I may fall back asleep and ask, *What are you trying to take?* I could pass this dream on until it sounds so different I don't recognize it as my own. I could be any animal having this dream on a mobile. We dangle and spin in our own orbits. We tangle the lines holding us to the same larger cycle. Our felt bodies slap against each other, making little thuds.

8.

My sister watched *The Exorcist* in our brother's room. Her voice sounded like a secret as she described the possessed girl spider-walking backward down a set of stairs in her nightgown. The possessed girl's story is one of light pressing back against the darkness that distorts it. Years lie between my sister talking about this movie and my watching it, her saying and my seeing.

Two friends share the gray loveseat. Dave and I sprawl across the gold couch. A man rises in the bed of the pickup truck on the screen. He revs a chainsaw and wiggles his hips and we laugh. Two boys drive beside the pickup. The radio plays Oingo Boingo's "No One Lives Forever."

The popcorn is almost gone, crumbs and kernels swirl the red bowl. The milk glass may be poison. A friend warned me some vintage glass contains lead, which contaminates the food if the dish is scratched. On the screen, one character breaks another character's face with a rock in an abandoned train car. One friend looks away and says she will never come to movie night again.

I imagine a quiz that tells me which final girl I am: the blood-soaked woman screaming from the back of a red pickup; the woman standing in a swimming pool, fighting something only she sees; the woman who turns her back on a form risen from a mattress. Each says, in her own way, *I am not afraid.*

With his roommates, a boyfriend and I settled in on sinking sofas and thrifted chairs. Glassware drifted among us. Smoke hovered in the dark before the screen. PBR and High Life cans on a trunk coffee table; the leather speckled in cigarette ash, condensation-ring scarred. We watched the one where a band of criminals assault and murder two young women. The criminals hide out at a nearby house, not knowing at first that their hosts are one of the women's parents.

My boyfriend explained seeing the assault was vital to understanding the parents' brutal revenge. I pulled on one of his tee shirts, the cotton saturated with fryer oil from the restaurant where he cooked. I lit a cigarette and sat cross-legged on the twin mattress on the floor, the fitted sheet half off, ashes everywhere. By the time I stubbed it out, he was still holding forth on how horror reflects real life. His need to be right upset me more than the movie.

*

Three men and a woman stand on a cliff edge in a desert. It almost sounds like the start of a joke.

This more recent spin on the revenge trope sees a woman and a man in an affair on a getaway at the man's posh desert home. The mistress pads to the kitchen in an *I heart LA* shirt and bikini bottoms, blond hair flouncing. The rooms are warm with gold-pink light. She bites an apple and startles to see a man in hunting gear staring at her through a glass door. He's a friend of her boyfriend's, joined by another man. They observe her through the glass, transfixed expressions on their faces, as if they are at a zoo. It's hardly accidental. They are there to hunt.

My watching used to mostly include romantic comedies whose makeovers and choreographed prom dances softened obstacles the characters encountered, confrontations with popular class-mates, parents, best friends. I used to like fairy tales, myths, and folktales, their tendency to end: *And the moral of the story is...* The moral explains something horrible, longs to prevent it from happening, ever or again. The moral is a shorthand lesson. It encourages goodness and cautions against evil, greed, selfish-ness; advises the audience not to wander, want, or tempt.

The mistress's boyfriend feigns a call for the helicopter to come get her. The boyfriend reaches for her hand, encouraging her to wait at the house until the chopper arrives. He pushes her off the cliff. She lands on a tree. A dry gray branch pierces all the way through her.

*

My junior year of high school, my friends and I went to shows and swapped band shirts. We sat on hall floors before home-room, backs against lockers, leaned into each other's shoulders.

We piled pillows on my bedroom floor after school. One friend's boyfriend knew how to choke someone out. His girlfriend dem-onstrated—arms at her side, chin tucked to her chest. He stood behind her and hugged. Her head lurched toward the ceiling and she fell. Limp and still, she looked helpless on the floor as her boyfriend stood above her, staring. He turned to the rest of us watching what seemed private to them. He didn't smile but his eyes looked satisfied, a pleased and horrified sense of *What have I done?*

We had graduated from prank phone calls and Truth or Dare, ding-dong ditch and flashlight tag. Guessing the word a friend spelled out with a finger, letter by letter, on your back. Stories about girls with green ribbon chokers and escaped lunatics with hook hands. Ouija board séances, chants for Bloody Mary. Index fingers beneath someone stretched across the floor, whispering, *Light as a feather, stiff as a board*. The meanest friend added a little extra force when she slapped someone's skull and said, *Crack an egg on your head*. The stakes of ghost stories and creepy games rose when our bodies were part of them.

I knelt on the rug, arms at my sides. My friend's boyfriend stood behind me and squeezed. I felt the air leave me and none coming back. I pushed back in panic. He squeezed harder. My jaw clenched, gritting my teeth, and I fell. One pillow's navy blended into another's purple when I woke, face pressed into plastic trim, my cheek pebbled with bead prints. He offered to try again.

One night the mistress wants the men to dance. She shows them. Poolside in a short white dress, desert dark pressing in on the patio, a blue glow. She blasts the music.

I walked into the dark kitchen and the lights flicked on. My friends yelled, *Surprise*. My mother handed me an ad torn from the yellow pages. She'd rented a limo for my seventeenth birthday. My new boyfriend, friends, and I rode around Syracuse, snapping photos on disposable cameras. I saved the pale rectangle with the limo ad after the party.

*

I took an art elective in college. We studied value, drew blue jeans pinned to boards around the room. A half-circle of drafting tables arranged before each pair, the denim flashed with bright clamp lights. We all painted grocery store cupcakes or an Easter lamb cake. Then we each painted whatever we wanted.

A classmate lugged a bucket of rock salt into the studio near the end of the semester, mixed salt with paint on a palette, spread textured color across a canvas that looked complete to me. My classmate knew something I didn't, saw something I could not see.

*

I didn't regret the times we did, but I didn't want to again. I feared he'd take his love back. My joints locked on my twin bed. A carving sensation, stung and stretched. A sharpness. My stomach roiled. I was heavy, *stiff as a board* beneath him.

I split against the sounds he made. I entered a different atmosphere where the dark increased or decreased depending on where we were and the objects around us. Was there anything atop the dressers? Was the floor carpeted or bare wood? What was the finish? How high was the pile? Was the room clean or dirty? A child's room or an adult's room? How big was the bed? Was it a trick question if the answer is two stacked twin mattresses on a bunk frame? Could anyone hear? Who was in the other rooms? Would they say I let this happen and what would they call this? Were there curtains in the windows? Were they opened or closed? Were there streetlights outside? How many lit versus how many burnt out?

*

In the art class, we learned hues were more complex than what we squeezed from tubes. Red and blue had undertones. It was emphasized to lighten or darken the paints, add white, black, or some other shade to complicate each color the way shadows and light complicate them. I thought of jigsaw puzzles, how much sky pieces may resemble ocean pieces. How falling into a pattern can feel like making a routine, or hitting terminal velocity. How easy it becomes to say you're safe when you aren't or that someone loves you when they don't.

*

We went to his mother's house. Afternoon light pressed in on us making small talk with his mother and her boyfriend in a garage filled with benches and tools. My boyfriend showed me the room his mother kept for him in the house, though he no longer lived there. Wood-paneled walls, an unmade bed with flannel sheets. Refreshing the clothes in his backpack, he pulled a wallet-size photo from a dresser drawer to show me: his ex-girlfriend, a pink velour background like a halo around her long brown hair, silver cursive in one corner spelled the year, her name. Being in that room was the sound a character hears and follows to find neither ghost nor monster, but a stray cat who hisses and runs off.

*

Sun blared in the window. I had on a long-sleeve shirt with a tee over it: a band name in pink, five pistol barrels in semi-circle pointed at a smiling woman's face. My teacher asked if everything was okay when I turned in my quiz. I nodded and returned to my desk, sat there sweating. The waffle weave of my shirt-sleeves rubbed the cuts I'd made on my arm, the fabric irritated my skin. The window looked onto a manicured courtyard, other classrooms. No one ate lunch or did homework out there. No one crossed the courtyard to get to their next class. The maintenance—kept lawn, pruned trees—seemed functionally useless.

I cried after hanging up the phone the afternoon I broke up with him. It was spring. A movie played on the living room television.

A man and woman made out on the Manhattan Bridge as traffic sped by them.

The mistress gasps awake, coughing up blood. Ants crawl up and down the branch pressed through her. Ants crawl over her skin. Her blood drips to the sand, splatters the insects working there. She is no longer a mistress but a woman in the desert.

In an alternate ending, I said why I was leaving. The closest moment to closure was when he and I stood outside a spot where we used to hang out. I tried to talk about what happened between us. He tore his tee shirt from the hem to the collar and walked away, shirt halves flailing.

*

My appetite waned for days. I went to the hospital fatigued and nauseated. Taped to a cabinet, a laminated chart with a one-to-ten pain spectrum. Straight line for a mouth at 1. The face agonized to 10, an anguished, miserable frown showing *Worst pain possible*. The second time the needle slipped from my arm, the nurse bandaged the butterfly in place.

The woman in the desert hides in a cave and builds a small fire. She doses herself with peyote and cuts open a beer can. She heats the metal in the flames, presses it against the gash in her stomach. She burns the wound shut to stay alive.

A nurse wheeled an AV cart into my room. Safe in the small, clean space, I fell asleep during opening credits to a movie I didn't pick. I woke to a nurse pulling the needle from my hand, covering the pinprick with a Band-Aid.

*

Another thing I remember: No animals appear throughout the movie in which men plan to hunt. I don't recall a single bird flying across the sky.

*

Night, strange insects attached themselves to the parking lot fence, the porch lights. My mother and I were sitting on the front steps of our townhouse. The fence, the air, and the lines marking parking places buzzed humid and warm.

I was too sick to take final exams and my school scheduled make-ups. The proctor sighed each time I asked to use the bathroom.

I focused on each object in the exam room. The doctor said I should have said something, I should have come in sooner. The exam room objects had binary categories—white or silver, rectangular or round, shining or matte. That, this. Soft, firm. Paper, metal.

There's something inside of me that's lethal,[1] says the teenager who finds herself fanged beneath her skirt. It's not new—the myth of vagina dentata. A moral based on reciprocal violence, rather than a reasonable standard for human goodness.

I talked with a friend. She talked with someone else.

I became too small to fit my clothes but I saw myself in the mirror each day. So I didn't know what to say the first day of school when a teacher asked if I'd eaten anything over the summer. Familiarity is a pattern that eclipses the gradual fade, makes it easy to miss.

Comments appeared on my online journal, each indenting further right, so the lines wrapped around on themselves like a cruel poem. The anonymity deepened my hurt, my sense of who I might trust. The commenter who mentioned my cuts could have been the same one who suggested I make out with a firearm.

I've heard online posts endure forever, even deleted, cached some place. I haven't gone looking for them. Thinking of them flutters something embarrassed and immensely sad inside me.

I don't know the odds it takes to end up in a young women's group where another member knows who you're talking about. The guidelines we were given seemed simple: keep what was said at the circle table in the room with the closed door, refrain from naming names, use labels instead—a grandfather, a mother's boyfriend, a friend, a boyfriend.

I don't know if she meant it the evening she sat down at the circle table and said someone would be waiting in the parking lot to jump me after group. It was November. I called my mother when I was done, told her to call when she was parked outside because I was afraid to wait alone. The parking lot outside the waiting room's glass windows and doors didn't look dangerous; gold funneled down from tall streetlights, held the cars and the space around each of them safe.

*

I've heard *Speak up* said in a scolding way, sharpness in encouragement, edges like *Spit it out*. Like the whole of something larger is held up, suspended, in the air between having something to say and saying it. Like the language for everything that has ever happened exists. Any saying feels like he and I were, are, both on trial.

I am weary of morals as explanations, hard lessons, the idea of something to show for pain. I hear the word *tell*—as in *Tell your story*—and think of tattling, someone whining, *I'm telling*. I think of stories where animals and creatures stand in for people. The ways they hurt each other, held at the distance of fable, less real. The moral is there might not be a moral.

One assumption about a final girl being the person who lives to tell the story is that her survival is attached to telling; she is expected to say it, to tell, again and again; she can't live without a saying so revealing she is bare before the audience, the moment is bare.

*

On the back porch at night, I sat with my legs pretzeled on a green and white lawn chair, a coffee can to catch ashes and cigarette butts nested between my thighs. A neighbor parted her floor-length blinds to our shared patio. The long slats swayed and revealed a sliver of her face. My sadness on display felt embarrassing.

Cars on the road decreased the later it got. I watched the trickle slow. Like the headlights, images of dying started small and grew. They took up the space I did not, expanded like water freezing, breaking the shell of what contains it: ice tray, gutter, asphalt.

Erika L. Sánchez's poem "Six Months after Contemplating Suicide" holds despairing in-between-ness: *Admit it—/you wanted the end//with a serpentine/greed. How to negotiate//that strangling/*

mist, the fibrous//whisper?//To cease to exist/and to die//are two different things entirely.[2]

I thought in hypotheticals—*If the next car is red, I'll go inside. If the next car is blue, I'll have another cigarette. If the next car is gray... If the next car is green...* I swung between empty and overwhelmed, a gas tank that knows only how to sputter out or overflow.

*

A telekinetic teenager gets her period for the first time in the shower after gym. She runs for her clothed peers preparing to leave the locker room. She extends her bloody, wet hands, begging for help. Her classmates laugh at her. She falls to the tile floor, crying as menstrual products sail toward her. Her peers chant, *Plug it up!*[3] The refrain's underlying sentiment is familiar.

No drama was how my friends said it. The rule handed down from a strict council who met on hall floors, sharing cigarettes creekside, lying on a bed while talking on the phone.

Leslie Jamison writes: *I think dismissing wounds offers a convenient excuse: no need to struggle with the listening or telling anymore.* Plug it up. *Like somehow our task is to inhabit the jaded aftermath of terminal self-awareness once the story of all pain has already been told.*[4]

We permitted only so much pain. The kind in our favorite songs—heartache, parents who are too distant, parents who are too close, feelings of placelessness. It was considered dramatic to play the sad song a second time, to live in a feeling, again and again, like a rock one was trying to identify. Wounds had to be surface-level, in need of a Band-Aid, not sutures. Mollified by, *That sucks*. No one wanted to see the bone.

The woman in the desert butchers the men. The telekinetic teenager sets fire to the senior prom. The teen with teeth inside her ditches her bike in the road and flags down an unsuspecting driver.

The origins of *revenge* are the Latin *vindicare*, to lay claim to, avenge, punish and a prefix denoting *back to the original place*.

In an earlier revenge film, a young woman meets three men in the woods as she's taking candles to church. The men assault and murder her, stealing her fine clothes. The men seek shelter at a farm, where the woman's family lives. The father finds his daughter's clothes. Before murdering the men, the father punishes himself. He goes for birch branches, presses his weight against the tree to bend the trunk. He tears the whole tree from the earth.

Revenge narratives often rely on someone harmed becoming as monstrous and violent as the person who harmed them. I am too soft to obliterate a tender self in favor of a cruel one.

*

If the body does not scar. If vitamin E is rubbed on a wound. If someone leaves an office is their file shredded? Did anyone take notes? Did it happen? What happens if someone keeps it to themselves? What happens if someone seeks care elsewhere—a new practice, a new city—and neglects to have files forwarded? How often do medical facilities shred files? How often does an internet cache empty? Where does it empty? Where do shreds go? Where do comments go? Does a cache show how many times someone refreshed a page to check for new comments? Does a cache know why anyone would keep searching? In what dark web place do the comments live? Can shame sear hot enough to vaporize someone to atomized particles? If the body does not scar, where does the event go? How is it recorded? What happened?

*

The telekinetic teenager slams windows closed with her mind. Her mother swears her daughter has Satan's power, but the girl corrects her: *It's nothing to do with Satan, Mama. It's me. Me. If I concentrate hard enough, I can move things.*[5]

Nights I took long to fall asleep and nightmares frequented the rest. I often woke feeling like I hadn't slept at all, scratchy-eyed, skin like sandpaper, blood and muscles pressing outward.

An octopus may change the color and texture of its skin to blend with its surroundings and hide from predators, or to indicate its mental state—fear or joy or love.

More blood was drawn, studied on slides. Fearful I'd hear again I should have spoken up, I didn't tell the gastroenterologist I was referred to for additional tests.

A nurse bunched my shirtsleeve and explained the anesthetic. My mind would fall asleep enough to forget the procedure, but I'd be awake enough to follow directions, my body guided by someone else: breathe, swallow a scope so the doctor could image my stomach. Panic saturated me as I slipped along, unable to stop the mild sedation, poetically known as twilight anesthesia. The room trembled, as if heat hazy, but it was winter.

In the movie where a vengeful tooth fairy ghost appears in the dark and kills anyone who looks at her, a boy won't sleep in the dark. Doctors diagnose him with severe nyctophobia. They prescribe anti-anxiety pills and sensory deprivation in a dark, enclosed chamber.

The gastroenterologist suggested stress was making me sick.

Symptoms can be active scars where brain and body converge. A song raises fine, short hairs on the arms. A feeling unfurls as a heavy chest, a roiling stomach. A whiff of men's body spray— on a sidewalk, in the grocery store, at a bar—conjures the feel of a rollercoaster cart reaching the top of the first hill, preemptive weightlessness flourishing in the muscles, the split second of panic before something clicks and releases and the coaster train falls.

Remembering inflames a hollowing heaviness, a fist-size knot in my chest. In textbook figures highlighting the sternum, the shape resembles a necktie color-coded into three parts. The bottom region is the xiphoid process, a piece of cartilage that ossifies as a person ages into and through adulthood. It seems no mistake that *xiphoid* is a descendent of *xiphos*, Greek for sword.

9.

A headstone notes the dates someone lived. A scar is evidence an injury happened. A wound existed and healed. I study my scars. One on my thigh started as a mosquito bite when I was ten. I scratched so hard I broke the skin. My mother read ammonia would relieve the itch. She put some on a cotton ball and dabbed a few raised spots on my thigh. I felt dizzy from the burn and smell, like cat pee and perm chemicals. In the next days the skin blistered like a grapefruit peel, then calmed to pink. The quarter-size wound healed to a nickel-size scar. I tried tanning the mark, massaged lotions and creams onto it. It's faint now—a small island chain, a wine bottle, a uterus, an hourglass, a perfume decanter, a mushroom cloud. The shape changes depending on how I pull the skin and tilt my head. I put my finger on the place and smell ammonia.

*

I had not been before, flooded by a pressure I felt to relax. Yoga seemed useless if I could not quiet my mind. I brought a pilates mat from home, the surface nicked from my cat kneading the blue foam with her claws. My hands beneath me, chest and throat pulled toward the ceiling—fish. Flat on my back—corpse. I felt heavy, my chest lassoed, about to cry, not for physical discomfort or pain. Some deep ache welled up in me, opened or released. I didn't go back.

Months later, spraying melamine plates in the dish room at work, a coworker and I talked about yoga. I mentioned I almost cried. She said my body was trying to let go of something. *You don't need to carry that around.*

I used to imagine faxes and emails as wire-thin scrolls that bent and slid through the wires between telephone poles to reach a distant screen. I imagined wires run along the bottoms of lakes, rivers, and oceans. The paper running through the wires like checks and deposit slips clapped into cylinders to journey from a car to a teller through a bank's pneumatic tubes.

*

Aase Berg writes: *Poetry is a will to put things right, an imaginary solution, a way of avoiding a catastrophe that already happened. Poetry is an escape, perhaps intelligent, perhaps idiotic, from a senile situation. It is a dialectical movement, it keeps tearing open the wounds while trying to heal them.*[1]

Nothingness lived in my poems like a reflex. Like looking for a remote while holding it. Like pulling another cigarette from a pack and setting it on an armrest while I held one two-thirds burnt down. I did not notice until someone pointed it out in feedback. Scribbled fast and messy in a margin: *Stop with the nothing.* The word, a default for moments or feelings I would not name.

Nothing was a persona, a fill-in, an orb pulling me into it, a water vortex swirling down a drain—recognizable to anyone who has taken a bath, but private and specific to me watching it.

*

The arborist names several species on the back patio. Sugar maple, one—dead. Norway maple, one—alive with a scar up its trunk, remains of an ankle-high wire garden fence at the foot—a tree grown through wire. Ailanthus, one; the arborist says it is known as a *tree of heaven* and may become a problem because the roots will spread and spread.

The weed's leaves are bright green splashed with red feathered edges. I umbrella-fold the leaves to the stem and pull. The weed lifts a patio stone corner when it comes up. I press the stone down, afraid to look at first. I keep pulling. I reveal a network of ailanthus roots, white and tangled. I rip them all from the damp, sandy soil.

...it keeps tearing open the wounds while trying to heal them...[2]

Hacking off new growth inspires defense branches to grow. Like the movie with the cartoon mouse dressed in a red sorcerer's cloak and a pointy violet hat with white stars on it, a moon. Brooms multiply and water accumulates as the music tempo picks up. To annihilate an ailanthus, an online video tutorial instructs to drill a diamond-shaped pattern of holes in the tree trunk. Two people push mushroom plugs into the holes. The fungus will overtake the ailanthus. The tree will die within several seasons.

10.

Two teenagers sprawled across a green armchair and loveseat, mauve carpeting beneath the living room furniture. Flames crack in the fireplace. One says, *Are you gonna see James tonight?*

Her friend says, *Why are you suddenly so interested in who I'm gonna see at night? Nighttime is my time.*[1]

The air clouded with glass cleaner and sweat, the too-sweet strike of so many celebrity perfumes colliding. My hands gripped brass, I spun clumsily. I saw myself in the floor-to-ceiling mirror each dancer vamped along as she began her set, stretching into the panels, kissing her own face—elevated onstage, shielded by a rule that forbade patrons from touching the dancers.

*

Someone pulled me in his bedroom. I couldn't tell if the heat in my face was from drinking or wanting. He laid me down on the floor and stood over me, his hands held his waistband, as if making an assessment.

*

The bartender cautioned of raids and told us to stay on the patio. I smoked cigarettes at a picnic table, nervous we'd get caught. A friend and I drank cocktails that looked like liquid amethyst. I felt myself fray into the night. Dancing beside tables that looked like big empty thread spools, my skirt turned on my hips, the zipper and button on the side. I could hardly stand on the sidewalk. Someone carried my shoes.

I woke in the tub, wearing my underwear and tank top. I stumbled into the living room, noticed an aquarium tank with a snake. A heat lamp shined on the glistening scales. I wanted to leave, but my friend said we were drunk. Someone gave me a blanket and asked if I wanted to watch a movie. Someone told me I'd like it.

A clown at a roadside oddities shop emcees a murder ride featuring serial killers. Four travelers take it and learn of a notorious local legend. Intrigued by the lore, the travelers detour. They pick up a hitchhiker. A tire blows out.

The hours stretched shadow-long. I wanted morning, my own bed. The movie was still playing.

The villains dress two of the travelers in rabbit costumes, shove them into a coffin, and lower them into an underground tunnel system. Creatures tear open the coffin. A woman sheds her costume and runs through blue passages, a stretch lined with skeletons. She reaches a red-lit chamber where filthy people sit around with devices on their heads. A static-scratched television hums. Someone convulses on a grimy operating table.

I wanted water, but couldn't find a glass. My head throbbed as I stood in the kitchen. A bottle of Midori glowed bright green on the counter. The snake moved on its branch, the skin patterns bunched and elongated. I worried the snake would escape and swallow me. Was the humming I heard the sunlamp, the snake's hunger, my head? Was it bar neon dimming, the sweet-sick taste on my teeth, shower water beading on my body until the drops were full enough to speed down my skin, toward the drain?

*

We sat on the blue sofa in his apartment. He poured wine. In his bedroom, he stopped kissing me to ask my confirmation name. I said I didn't have one. He kissed me more. Driving home, I saw a group of deer cross the road by the Westcott Reservoir. Two in the morning and mine was the only car on the street. I stopped to watch them, ambling and graceful. Alert eyes, sweet faces. I let him photograph me for a school project in my basement bedroom at my mother's. A coffee can of cigarette butts beside my bed, a twin mattress supported by plastic storage totes. I had conflicting concerns: he was too good for me or he wasn't all that nice. I thought if he saw where I lived I wouldn't have to tell him I was afraid, he'd lose interest. He sent me the pictures, asked to see me again. I said I was busy.

The woman cradling a log like an infant—sage-like and prophetic—meets the girl's hopelessness with empathy. She puts her palm to the teenage girl's forehead, as if feeling for a fever, and says, *When this kind of fire starts, it is very hard to put out. The tender boughs of innocence burn first and the wind rises and then all goodness is in jeopardy.*[2]

I sometimes felt afraid heading home—on a bus or walking, digging in my purse to find keys. I was not afraid as I dressed and put on makeup, nor as I walked to the parties or moved through them. I felt safety in repetition, even as I echoed my mistakes.

*

I rewatched the movie with the murder ride, rabbit costumes, and underground chambers. I wanted to know how it ends. A hand emerges from earth and dry grass in morning. The hand becomes an arm, then a woman in a little-girl's dress—blue and short with a doll collar, fabric dirty and blood-streaked. She stumbles to the road. She waves an arm from a torn sleeve, signals an approaching car. The car picks her up. She says she needs a doctor. The driver—the murder-ride emcee without costume or makeup—says, *I'll get you to a doctor.*[3]

*

We watched *Shaun of the Dead* with his friends. We were sleepy, warm, and slow after they left the room. The next morning, he said, *You're still here?* returning from the shower, to find me still in bed. Staying was a breakfast invitation without asking. I felt embarrassed I wanted his company, sad I knew the answer. Everything that was going to happen between us had happened.

I descended the quiet stories alone from his room at the top of the house. I stepped over cups and cans on the stairs, went out the heavy front door. Headed to my dorm, I passed clusters of parents and prospective students scattered across campus, tour groups with bright orange bags. I had on jeans and a red tee shirt with small white flowers, black ballet flats. I could have been headed to brunch, the library. I asked myself if it was a walk of shame if I was not wearing painful heels or something short. Was it a walk of shame if I was not sorry until I was outside the house.

Halloween and pajama parties. Playboy Mansion parties. CEOs and office hoes. Graffiti parties where we wore white clothes and drew on each other. Short shorts and miniskirts. Decade parties for the roaring '20s, pop-bright '80s, and grungy '90s. Saints and Sinners. Black light parties. I saw many toga-draped forms on Syracuse streets and sidewalks, faux-olive-leaf-crowned gods and goddesses on campus buses late at night, going wherever, but I never attended a toga party. I borrowed a pink polo shirt and a skirt from a friend for golf pros and tennis hoes. We chewed mushrooms on a boys' floor of the dorm, passed vending machine orange juice between us because we heard we'd feel it sooner. I went to a spin-the-bottle party and didn't kiss anyone.

The *Splat Pack* refers to directors who work on minimal budgets and create abundantly violent films, occasionally dismissed as torture porn. Among them: Rob Zombie, Eli Roth, James Wan, Robert Rodriguez, Alexandre Aja. No women were canonized in the initial Splat Pack.

*

What was I doing in those rooms is another way to ask what I wanted to prove. I knew the difference between something regretted and something unwanted. Maybe I felt worthless. Maybe I liked it. I made room for my want and sometimes wanted more. I felt sad not to hear from some people again and wondered who felt the same to not hear from me.

Veterinary school students haze first-years, including a girl whose older sister attends the same program. The sisters were raised vegetarians. Eating a rabbit liver in a hazing ritual awakens meat cravings in the younger sister. Bright blood splattered across a dull palette. Her appetite intensifies—a gas station sandwich, raw chicken, human flesh. Her body endures untamable urges and grisly reactions, the consequences of satisfying such intense want.

His apartment was behind the dorm where my friends lived. His roommates gone for Thanksgiving break, he picked me up and put me on the counter beside the stove.

Colorful lights, thumping music. The sisters attend late-night dance parties where everyone's energy collides. It's familiar: the light and sweat, beer blurred with waving arms and crushed red cups. Puffs of smoke becoming contrails above everyone's head before disappearing.

I took a bus in a snowstorm to meet up with someone at a bar. We went to his place, where he put on a DVD. Neon silhouettes of women danced to techno on the screen. Drinking Wild Turkey, we walked around the apartment in our underwear for an hour before he touched me.

I had on a blue flowy top of hers, spaghetti straps and small flower appliques sewn on the neckline. My black dorm-cut hair choppy and teased. He walked between us across campus, offered each of us a hand and swung our arms.

*

The Splat Pack is not as familiar a horror concept as final girls and scream queens.

The younger sister puts on a dress and lipstick. She dances before a mirror, her headphones blaring like an electric pulse. She kisses her reflection, the shot taken as if from inside the mirror.

From the row behind ours, a stranger said, *You two are so lucky. I want what you have.* She didn't know we were friends. We made out on the side of a house, and the year before we played Guitar Hero in his friend's dorm room and watched *Sleepaway Camp* in the lounge, got stoned behind the dorm. We weren't in love or anything like it. An incision of blue light sliced beneath my roommate's door. When I walked him out the next morning, my roommate was making breakfast in our kitchen. I put on coffee and she told me she was worried.

A friend said, *Just because someone wants to have sex with you, doesn't mean you should.* We were in a bar after class, the evening before I took a flight to see an ex. Or we were smoking between dances in a strobe-lit basement. Or we were fixing our hair and reapplying lip stain in a bathroom. It's not that she told me on more than one occasion. She said it once and I thought of her caution often. I believed her and still my want welled up, overflowed.

The younger sister and her father sit at the breakfast table. He says, *Your mom was tough at first.*[4] He unbuttons his shirt to reveal his scarred chest, the skin monstrously ruffled. She sees she was born into her hunger, a deep bodily longing.

*

He said the party was too hot. We were in a dark kitchen and he opened the fridge, sat on a shelf. He held on to me while we kissed, unbuttoned my jeans. I pulled away, looking at everyone else in orbits of oblivion and want. He wrote an address on a paper scrap, pressed it into my palm. His friend wanted to come with us. I said okay and caught a bus home. I didn't see him again.

The camera like a satellite empathizes with the two teenage girls. The living room shot from above. One asks: *Do you think that if you were falling in space that you would slow down after a while or go faster and faster?*

Her friend says, *Faster and faster. And for a long time, you wouldn't feel anything. And then you'd burst into fire, forever. And the angels wouldn't help you because they've all gone away.*[5]

I said someone could stay but I was going to sleep. In my bed, he put his hand down my pants and sloshed against me. I faced the wall and he bucked against my back, my pajama pants and underwear the difference between our skin. In other contexts, this was a thing. Someone else liked it—feeling each other through fabric, wanting closely distant. I didn't want that night though. I didn't want him. I said it wasn't going to happen and went to sleep on the living room couch, half-awake most the night, staring at his motorcycle helmet on the coffee table. In the morning, perched on the track of the sliding door off the living room, I smoked cigarettes, waiting for him to leave. The sun was hot. I was thirsty. I stared into the wide pit behind my apartment. The pit had a reputation. Deer grazed, feral cats stalked. Grass and weeds overgrew with abandon until someone on a riding mower breezed through the crater.

Someone paused and told me to take a deep breath before touching me again. In the seconds between the inhale and him, I didn't know what was about to happen. I trusted him. I wanted him. My breath pulled deep, waiting to feel what he would do.

Gifts spill across a credenza, pastel paper and bows, soft ribbons on pink bags. A deer grazes in the yard. I'm moved by her gentle trudging through the snow, how she picks at dry branches to feed herself, how smoothly she walks down the sloping hill where the house sits, and slips through the trees.

Face shellacked in recital makeup. Hair pinned in a bun. I sat in the back seat, riding home for a snack between matinee and evening shows. My mother slowed the car, annoyed, *That dog is out of control.* A white car crawled before us. A wide, not-human shape overwhelmed the heads in the back seat. Slowing more, my mother said, *That's not a dog.* A deer rolled out the back windshield, landed in the road and stood. Red and pink insides hung from one side like garland. The deer staggered across a church lawn, a shrine to the Virgin Mary, to the trees. The white car pulled over. We did, too. My mother checked on the people, a family headed to Old Country Buffet for Mother's Day lunch. Watching my mother leaned to the driver's window, I worried the deer would come back and jump in our car next. The people shook in their seats, according to my mother, covered in glass pieces, tufts of fur, red flecks and smears.

The campus apartment parking lots emptied. The student center dimmed on its limited winter break hours. My roommate went home. My second night alone, I heard a noise at the sliding back door. I sat on the stairs debating whether to look, whether smoking one cigarette inside would set off the smoke alarm, whether my roommate's several-week absence was long enough for the smell to disappear. I opened the blinds to two deer at the glass, looking in the living room, their faces gentle and curious. Mine was the only light on along the block.

Dave and I drove to Buffalo for a show. He helped with load-in and we ate dinner at a tiki restaurant near the venue. The show went late. I fell asleep on the ride home and woke to my body jolting, my head hitting the window. Thinking I'd felt the car coast onto the rumble strip, I said, *Did you fall asleep?* Eyes fixed on the road, Dave said, *I hit a deer.* The passenger mirror dangled from a few thin wires. We pulled over and got out to look. The deer had run off and we were beyond it anyway. Dave pulled the broken mirror from the car. I stayed awake on deer watch the rest of the way home. I saw more between the trees. I wondered what happened to ours. I went back and forth on who hit whom and what it meant for all involved in the collision.

My sister and I rolled cookies and crackers into sleeping bags. Early morning, we dragged our parcels out to the tree house our father built in the backyard. Light wood beams structured into two tiers. We sat on the top level and snacked, watching the golf course beyond the fence. Some mornings, deer crossed the grass before carts carrying men, bags, and clubs arrived. The deer paused and bent to bushes, rested beside the tree line, as if the acres belonged to them.

I left a friend's house late at night. Deer stood beneath the four-way light near my apartment. Walking home from class with a friend another evening, a deer leapt from a row of bushes.

*

My eyes feel sandpapery as we slog through the crowded venue, out to frosty night air, our car. I stay awake on the drive home. I watch for deer on the roadside and the white deer at the army depot, a rare herd with a recessive gene that exhibits completely white fur. The white deer live protected in fenced parameters, safe from hunters and cars. I focus on the fence, fit my eyes into each metal diamond. I breathe lightly, so not to fog the window. We're going fast, but I see one. Spectral and brief: white descending, folding knees to dry, cold earth beside the fence, ghostly and bright, close enough that—if we stopped, if I got out of the car—I could put a finger through the fence and feel softness. The car slowing would not be enough. I want to feel the coarse white fur pressed through the fence; this to me is evidence of a human instinct to keep safe those who need safe-keeping—our readiness to admire and protect an animal equally as threatened by the car wreck it can cause, vulnerable to human encroachment: drivers, hunters, tourists, developers.

Animals pulse through the snow during a blizzard. The four men visiting the cabin behold from the porch. Wave after wave of fur and feathers through thick snow. Wildlife fleeing danger may be a natural indicator of pending disaster.

An organization devoted to saving Seneca white deer offers thirty-dollar depot tours. Tourists, animal lovers, military enthusiasts, naturalists, and families take guided expeditions through the fenced-in enclosure. As on a whale watch, seeing white deer is not guaranteed with admission, but the organization encourages photos: *This is your opportunity to see the hidden world and experience the magic of the white deer yourself.*[1]

Whitetail deer antlers are deciduous. They shed and grow back annually. Growth begins in spring—small, soft nubs protrude. The nubs calcify and grow, developing through the summer. Velvet covers the antlers, a fine plush hosting veins and capillaries that carry blood, nutrition, and oxygen up the rack. The velvet is sensitive, attuned to spatial arrangement, like cat whiskers. The antlers stop growing in fall. The capillaries stop supplying blood to the velvet and the tissue dies. The deer rub their antlers against trees to shed their velvet. Eventually, the antlers fall off, too. A new set grows the following spring, the cycle repeats.

Deer shedding velvet appears gruesome and painful, but the velvet falling off is a relief.

In photos, deer gnaw the dangling shreds that fall near their mouths. They head-butt trees as if fighting the trunks. The bark is a tool for scratching off the itchy flesh. Their instinct to gnaw and rub is its own language. Red interior exposed, a macabre chandelier, shed pieces flail on a rack.

*

In sixth-grade reading class, we read *Where the Red Fern Grows* by Wilson Rawls to study narrative arc. The climactic scene sees Billy take his hounds on a night hunt. The dogs tree a mountain lion that attacks and gravely injures Old Dan. Billy rushes his dogs home, where his mother washes Old Dan's intestines and stitches them back inside the dog. Old Dan dies of infection; Little Ann follows soon after with a broken heart. I read the mountain lion chapter so many times, like restarting a song as soon as it ends because I needed to hear it again. Reading it I felt like all the hair on my head had grown inward and was vining around my brain.

*

Our first wedding anniversary, Dave and I carried a picnic to a local cemetery, now a city park. The local historical society hosts an annual 5K on the path that winds by the tombs. Volunteers pick up litter monthly, wash and care for the markers, restore what they can save. A volunteer and visitor presence reduces vandalism. People are less likely to tag a vault or push fallen stones into the creek or steal slabs with other people nearby.

Our four-year wedding anniversary, we go to Brooklyn to visit the Morbid Anatomy Museum, a brick building painted black, the name in sharp white letters at the top. We've come to see the "Taxidermy: Art, Science, and Immortality" exhibition, which includes Victorian taxidermist Walter Potter's famed tableau "The Kittens' Wedding," borrowed from the current owner on crowd-sourced funds.

The first floor is a gift shop and café. Giant mounted animal heads hang in the upstairs entryway. Beneath them, I read the curator's statement from J. D. Powe and Evan Michelson:

...The objects on display here are witness to the fact that one era's cultural norm often becomes incomprehensible over time. What never changes is the strange, persistent, uniquely human desire to simultaneously destroy and immortalize those things we seek to understand, and those things we love.[2]

I weave through the room filled with wall-mounts and glass boxes: a giant lobster claw, fish, ornamental glass boxes with pet dogs inside, age-toned ribbons tied in perfect bows around their necks. I imagine the dogs sitting fireside with someone they love, fingers offering a scrap, a calling voice, a gentle hand brushing back the fur.

A wide glass case in the center of the room holds a smaller case inside: tiny crafted shoes; a disgruntled-looking kitten guest toward the back of the scene—the mouth turned up and slightly frayed at the corners; a maybe-mother-of-the-bride looking on with care and concern, ruched and lacy dress bodices; blue and red beady necklaces; ballet-pink noses; delicate earrings in turquoise, red, pearl; the smallest kitten dressed in a sailor suit, one paw on the altar railing; the reverend presiding, one paw turned up toward the heavens and another holding open a prayer book with very tiny words handwritten on the pages; a breadcrumb-size ring on the bride's finger, the train of her ivory gown; the groom's tabby head tilted adoringly.

I stand on each side awhile and study the astonishing details. Nineteen kittens, wavy in their postures, like birds or sea lions. Many of the front paws seem unsure what to do with themselves. Every guest wears a different expression—most stoic and watchful; two with bright blue eyes look surprised.

An online image search for *kitten wedding* yields the tableau from various angles. Theories and backstories about the wedding guests change, depending on where a spectator stands.

The search also shows: wedding shoes with kitten heels; kittens wearing veils on their heads, garters on their necks like frilly collars; wedding cakes with cat toppers; Badgley Mischka, Carolina Herrera, fake-pearl-and-gem-studded high heels with red sticker soles adhered to look like Louboutins; a kitten in a bunk bed; just-married couples kissing and holding kittens; a black-and-white photo of wedding-attired kittens, a bell on white ribbon; a kitten in a hammock; rabbits at school desks, little chalkboards between their paws; Tyco's '90s Kitty Kitty Kittens dolls; a teapot with a hand-painted kitten on it; kittens stepping on sample invitations.

What never changes is the strange, persistent, uniquely human desire to simultaneously destroy and immortalize those things we seek to understand, and those things we love.[3]

People wrap pets in their favorite towels or blankets, say good-bye, send them into rooms with technicians or veterinarians who send the pets into the beyond. People tell their pets goodbye, hold their paws. People hire pet hospice to administer euthanasia in their living room. People have passed-on pets cremated—group cremation or the more costly individual service, so they're assured the only ashes in the urn belong to their pet and no one else's. People keep urns on mantels or bars. People have taken pet ashes on vacation to Fogo Island to scatter a dusting at Brimstone Head, one of the four corners of the world, according to the Flat Earth Society.

Other options exist to memorialize a dead pet, consolations and reminders for every budget.

You can bury your pet in your backyard—in a shoebox, a Sephora box, with their favorite toy or treat, a poem, a lock of your hair. You can bury your pet in a biodegradable urn and, assuming you do not move your residence, you may enjoy the tree eventually, someday. You can send a carefully measured tablespoon or two of cremains to companies like Gem-Pet or LifeGem or Cremation Solutions; after enough months, you will receive a gemstone in the mail—cubic zirconia, diamond—and a certificate. The stone's shade is determined in the machine and depends on the ashes' carbon content. You may have the gemstone set in a paperweight, necklace, or ring. Dazzle grief into shine. You can order a custom hand-painted pet portrait necklace for $850. You can ask Theresa Furrer of Nine Lives Twine to spin your cat's or dog's fur into yarn. Or send your pet to space with Celestis Pet, whose expeditions carry pet cremains as cargo. Depending on how much you pay, your pet may be returned to earth, to you, or your pet may take *a permanent celestial journey*.

A father buries the dead family cat in sacred ground with resurrecting powers. The cat who returns to life is nothing like their pet, but instead a spitting, hissing, scratching approximation crawled from the earth.

A pet may be cloned to duplicate something like their presence. A tissue specimen gets shipped to a company like ViaGen Pets to start the replication process. A vet may take a biopsy and preserve it ahead of time, though ViaGen's website also offers instructions on obtaining a sample from a just-deceased pet.

Beside himself after his son's death, the father considers burying the boy in the special dirt. His neighbor who showed him the place cautions: *Sometimes, dead is better.*[4] Which is another way of saying grief can beget a desperate reaching whose longing occludes logic.

*

Someone left a piece of paper with a heart on the cat's body, a small flower bouquet in the paws. The cat was not ours, but it's on the corner of our street and the day is warming.

All the boxes we have are enormous, left over from a move. Dave takes a silver contractor bag and garden gloves. I kiss my cats and head out, calling our vet for advice. The vet's office suggests burial, cremation, or calling county health. On the corner, Dave is deciding how to shift the cat into the bag. The cat could be rolling in a sun patch, but I don't want to look.

I call county health and a messaging service answers. They recommend I call the highway department. I picture men wearing bright orange vests, tossing dead animals into trash compactors. I want something gentle to help the cat pass softly into death. I call the vet back for the cremation price. The amount is uniquely specific—group cremation: $123.12.

Dave returns with the sagging bag and goes knocking on doors. A man answers at the first house, mid-breakfast cook, and says he and his family care for a wandering gray tabby. Dave comes home and takes a picture of the cat on my phone because his phone's memory is full. He emails himself the image, deletes it from my phone because he knows it will upset me. He shows the man the picture. The cat is his, the stray he calls Long Straw. Before Dave walks the bag down the street, I ask if the cat *just looks like he's sleeping*.

Dave says, *Sleeping with its mouth opened. Like howling in its sleep. Not peaceful.*

12.

The fog swallows itself and reveals a person. The mask is lifted.

I imagine my home without skulls and framed butterflies, a New Orleans alligator head, taxidermy books, dried flowers, deer ribs a friend found and brought over in a plastic grocery bag. I sat on a sun porch, wearing purple elbow-length dish gloves. I scrubbed the bones in a solution of water and hydrogen peroxide. I envision replacements, objects in the places of my own: throw pillows printed with wine jokes or mustaches; faux gold fruit; framed prints about life, love, and laughter. It doesn't sound like home.

I want to set a better example for myself. I hear everything waking up and could join or distance.

Morbid originates from the mid-seventeenth-century Latin *morbidus*, from *morbus*, meaning diseased.

Maybe I indulge what I should resist, cling instead of cure. Bones, unbreathing flowers, a cartoon Loch Ness Monster print, insects framed in flight. I am filling some part of myself that is eternally voided.

Curious derives from mid-fourteenth-century Latin, suggesting eager to know… often in a bad sense.

A curio cabinet displays object collections, sometimes strange or macabre, yet revered for those qualities.

Days stretch out and I am still but exhausted, my head spinning out against itself, a cabinet of all past dreads. The black reels over me like shark eyes rolled back, *the poem's hour of birth*[1] before I knew what a poem was. When the language I had to name it was a mangled strangeness—*The Four-Day Win*.

Morbid curiosity is eagerness to know disease, longing to know death without dying. It may be a way I grieve. It may be a way I pass the feeling through until I can stand it.

I search the phrase *four-day win*. The results aren't monsters or spirits. Not childhood depression or anxiety, but a title: *The Four-Day Win: End Your Diet War and Achieve Thinner Peace*. A diet may not be entirely unlike coping with depression or anxiety, or grieving: worksheets from a book, reviews, success stories, refrains of *I tried everything*.

I could be cast in navy light, looking out a window for the masked man behind me. I could be nodding off in a bubble bath as a razor glove rises like a shark fin from the foam.

13.

A boy in my fifth-grade class bragged he watched *Faces of Death*. He did not describe specifics, only that the movie was bloody and real and had anyone else seen it. No one else had. And no one really seemed to care.

A mailbox shaped as a tooth at the end of an East Syracuse driveway signals a family dentist. I have passed the tooth mailbox and felt my middle plummet, knowing a few seconds later I'd pass the house where a man built an underground concrete bunker to imprison and abuse women he abducted.

Playing in the grass outside our father's apartment, my sister and I met two girls whose mother lived in the complex. One sister took us to her hideout beneath the stairs connecting two apartment blocks. She pawed the dirt with her hands, unburied something shallow. I watched, curious, as she brushed dirt off a glass jar, revealing a dead bird she'd found. She said we could come back each week to check on it.

Considering a trip to Los Angeles, I found the Museum of Death among notable attractions. The collection features artwork by serial killers, a recruitment video and ephemera from the Heaven's Gate cult—a bunk bed, Nike sneakers, a shroud. *Traces of Death* plays footage of deaths on a loop. The displays are known to cause *falling down ovations*,[1] which means visitors pass out.

I see the museum's sibling on Dauphine Street in New Orleans a few years later. Tourists pause on the sidewalk to photograph show-bulbs that spell *MUSEUM OF DEATH* behind windows. None of us go inside. Wandering back to the French Quarter one evening, I pass a ghost tour every twenty feet. Enthusiastic guides point out buildings and alleys. They tell stories. Dave and I tour St. Louis Cemetery No. 1 with Save Our Cemeteries, a nonprofit whose mission is to *preserve, protect, and promote historic cemeteries of New Orleans through restoration, education, and advocacy*.[2] Our guide leads us around for two hours. He weaves New Orleans history with stories of those who fill the caveaux. He says we'll see hair accessories on the path or set on tombs throughout the cemetery. People leave them as small, subtle offerings. I tear out a few strands of my hair and set them on a tomb. I do not ask for anything.

Faces of Death was marketed as a found-footage film, but it's composed of reenactments. The boy in my class saw *Faces* and believed the reenactments were authentic, or he watched *Traces* and mistook the name. It would make more sense if the names were reversed—*Faces* showing real deaths, *Traces* depicting reenactments.

My classmates and I were less fascinated than the boy seemed to desire. His voice sounded hopeful, he so wanted to convince us he had seen people dying. No one avoided him, but no one asked about it either. We stayed busy with whatever else we were doing—coloring, fording digital rivers along the Oregon Trail, feeding lettuce to the class guinea pig.

A classmate fell during recess, scraped his knee on a sewer grate. No one was allowed to get close. We watched from the small hill that dipped from the school down to the playground. We watched from the tops of slides and black rubber swings dangling from chains. We watched from cracks in the tire tunnel, the skin on our arms pocked by playground gravel. A teacher and a nurse helped the boy. By the end of the school day, everyone swore the bone was showing. That night, I wrote about it in my ballerina diary. I emphasized my disgust by adding extra w's to the word *ew*. I drew a diagram of the boy's knee bone emerging from flesh. The bone was cartoony, round on one end. The torn skin flat like a piece of paper, jagged as a jack-o-lantern's smile.

The boy's knee wasn't on the local news or in the papers. The knee had no hashtag. A few days passed and we stopped talking about the bone, the skin, the blood. We stopped approaching the grate to look for red smears.

It's no longer the case. Life is poetry: ...*it keeps tearing open the wounds while trying to heal them*.[3] It's possible to bear witness to most newsworthy unfoldings, often in real-time. Screens insert us into tragedy and allow distance. We get closer, but not too close.

*

Someone dies by suicide and on social media I read monologues about depression, anxiety, substance abuse. Status updates stake claim to hopeful lives born from hopelessness. Comments voice shared experiences, surprise, support. People share reminders to check-in. They say they are there for anyone who needs to talk. They send thoughts and prayers. Asking *How are you feeling* isn't painful. Staying open to the honest answer can be heartbreaking. I want specific care conveyed beyond general refrains, echoes repeated until they sound so distant, they could be mistaken for background noise. A passing car, a plane crossing the sky.

*

If grief had an odor, it might smell like electricity, a battery felt through a phone, hot in the hand, instead of the deceased's hair or perfume, their skin. Grief has updated to match digital pace. Collective mourn seems both intimate and impersonal—overwhelming sadness seen while maintaining privacy. Not like calling someone to talk. Not like being at a wake or funeral. Not like going to therapy or a support group. The pain resides someplace else—a screen, a signal, a frequency. We drop off projections of our grief and harvest condolences when we log in again.

I have not yet mourned my dead on social media, even though I know grief has long been something to display and show. The personal-private tension of stepping up to "the veil" while existing among the living; being two places at once; catching a glimpse of the void and remaining. I think of widows dressing in black clothes and veils. I think of mourning jewelry—a loved one's hair braided with seed pearls, framed and displayed in a ring. The jewelry is both a reminder of who has died and the wearer's mortality.

The dead may get buried more than one place: interred in earth, immortalized in screen-bright elegies. Online obituaries reveal details of a life and death, survivors, service announcements. Readers respond with condolence comments, thoughts and prayers. They light candles, digital gold flames waving on the screen. They send flowers, pixelated white lily petals or live arrangements ordered online and delivered to the memorial service. They make donations *in lieu of flowers* in the deceased person's name. Facebook will memorialize accounts upon request.

Twitter will deactivate them. Instagram will either memorialize or deactivate an account. Disappear or join the social media graveyard. Social media pages, storage clouds, document files, inboxes, profiles, and accounts make up a person's digital estate.

Poetry, too, is a place where grief is publicly and privately endured, evolving line by line, or poem by poem. Muriel Leung's "Mourn You Better" poems appear throughout her collection *Bone Confetti*. Each segment in the series refracts and re-inspects grief's ever-changing nature. Early lines grasp toward normalcy in the face of grief: *Surrender to the cherry nothingness of go back/to the everyday. Like a runaway gurney I should/lie awake for a pink comet to engulf me.*[4] And later: *I am so good at saying the thing,/the generous hole and ballooning throat.*[5] The lines illuminate shifts in the speaker's mourning as the series progresses.

Mourning is elastic and necessary, and not exclusive to death. I remember a version of it in which I tried to build a shatter-proof self, fortified by self-destruction. I wished for a save, light to crack the ceiling, sharpness softened to gentle curves. All clock hands on morning when the day was too new to ruin.

I had this image of myself...[6]

I am looking for a balance between mourning and moving on. How does it look to not be so enamored with the image of the final girl—the one who survives—that we forget, or disavow, our dead (selves).

*

In 1918, a Syracuse munitions factory operating on a former limestone quarry exploded. The only structure still standing is a giant stone crusher, known among locals as the Crusher. The name has a mythic aura—violence with a whisper hushing the middle, like a torture device or annihilating force.

People rarely described the structure as existing in the same place. The Crusher seemed to move around the city and suburbs, one small stretch of underdeveloped acreage to another— ghosts, explosives, smoke, and all. My brother talked about the Crusher and another place, Lost Lake, as if they existed on the golf course behind our house, nighttime party spots for high school kids.

A friend told my sister and me the Split Rock Quarry was behind the apartment complex where she and her mother lived. Our mothers drank coffee on a caramel-colored sofa. My sister and I followed our friend. We walked through trees to a wide place, muddy and rocky. Big puddles spotted the landscape. We put our hands in the water; it clouded with dirt. We scooped jars through the water to collect tadpoles. They swam from our fingers, their tails writhing like ribbons. I was disappointed we did not hear the rumored hum of machinery. We saw no looming structure, no ghosts. This was not the Crusher.

I watch a video someone posted of Lost Lake online—a spring day, leaves not yet grown on trees, the grass yellow-green and dead, patched with exposed dirt; the lake water looks warm at the surface, frigid underneath. A drone flies over the landscape, through air I imagine smells mud-fresh and thawing, wet and possible. A slow, upbeat synth track scores the March or April cusp of Upstate New York—spring arriving at last on the tail of several last-ditch snow bursts.

The Morbid Anatomy Museum and Museum of Death are curated to accommodate the pain that fills them. The Crusher is scarred geography transformed by real-life horror.

Dark tourism describes visits to places familiar with death and tragedy. The visits expand a haunted house glimpse to a long stare into the dark.

New Orleans tour companies offer hybrid ghost tours and paranormal investigations. Participants borrow ghost-hunting equipment—camcorders, meters, EMF pumps, lights, recorders. French Quarter Phantoms, Bloody Mary's Tours, and Ghost City Tours offer investigations at places like historic homes, haunted pubs, and an infant asylum—all with expert guidance.

Horror movies are contained catastrophes. Dark tourism similarly connects a desire to look and feel afraid at the same time; it satisfies concurrent curiosity and repulsion, while preserving audience safety.

*

A Boomerang at the New York State Fair flung me into the almost-sky and the midway went dark. People were screaming. My chin fell to my chest. My eyes shut and my jaw locked. Two years later, I braced behind the safety bar on the Himalaya at the state fair. My hands gripped the silver metal so tightly my fingernails dug into my palms as the car plunged forward, coasted the track through a vinyl-curtained tunnel and back out to midway-night where people waited their turn. I loosened my grip on the bar when the car slowed and the ride nearly stopped. The cars pulled backward and I let go. My head fell back. I felt both there and not. Blacking out on intense amusement park rides may be the body's response to distress, fight or flight—terror held alongside physical sensations of being tossed, feeling weightless.

A neighbor, a kid in my grade, took my sister and me to the Crusher. Tall, graffitied, a dark tunnel on each side. I barely walked into a passage before I ran back out saying I couldn't. We climbed the back and peered down to a pit enclosed by Crusher walls. Spray paint implied someone had been in the pit, though I saw no way out of it. I felt anxious I might fall in, something might crawl up the wall. Cutting along the path home, the neighbor cautioned my sister and me that a hermit with a shotgun collection lived in the woods. My sister and I walked faster. Our mother grounded us when she asked what we did that day; she forbade us from going back. Teenagers partied there, she said. Satanic cults sacrificed animals in the tunnels. And I read online or my mother said it to scare me, but some source, reliable or not, said if I walked deep enough into the dark passages, I'd find animal intestines strung on the rotting wood rafters.

Beauty and devastating loss distinguish places like Aokigahara, Ithaca gorges, and the Golden Gate Bridge—naturally gorgeous panorama dotted with some dark knowing.

Reminders of nature's devastating potential are hardly scarce in our climate crisis. Storm-wrecked amusement parks with foliage flourished along rollercoaster tracks, paint-peeled snack shacks, boarded-up arcades. Neighborhoods with trees grown through abandoned houses.

Closed facilities carry human suffering and pain—hospitals, prisons, psychiatric treatment centers—some of which open each fall for guided tours, synchronized with Halloween.

The Whaley House, the Winchester Mystery House, and the LaLaurie House are museums, tourist attractions devoted to their ghosts. They torque the darkness and violence that changed them and display it as curiosity. Funding and committees assure these houses undergo necessary repairs and restoration. They're preserved in the interest of history.

Some places seek renaissance. The Amityville Horror House has been owned and inhabited by several families since the DeFeo family murders in 1974. One owner updated the attic's quarter-circle windows that made one side of the house seem to stare. One owner registered a different address with the postal service. Each change an attempt to ward off tourists or a bad feeling the owners got each time they wrote out 112 Ocean Avenue. The address no longer exists.

One version of Winchester Mystery House lore: Sarah Winchester, heiress to a rifle fortune, felt conflicted by her wealth, which cost others their lives. Following the deaths of her husband and child, she hoped to lift the curse she felt upon her by purchasing, and continuously renovating, a California home. This, she thought, would appease spirits who might protect her when she died. She allegedly hosted nightly séances to ask the spirits what they wanted. The result is a seven-story mansion abounding with strangeness: staircases to ceilings, spiderweb patterns, doors leading nowhere, a windowed floor. Thirteen repeated: windowpanes, ceiling panels, chandelier bulbs. Built into the Winchester Mystery House is a story as concerned with architecture, ghosts, and dark whimsy as it is with faith—a woman's belief that this was what she needed to do; glass, wood, nails, passageways, and spires could unburden her of what she knew to be real.

*

Several college students backpacking through Europe find themselves in a horrifying operation; people pay large sums to torture and kill captured travelers in an abandoned factory. The film hyperbolizes dark tourism, literalizes the *tourist trap.* Wealthy "hunters" travel from all over the world to indulge horrific fantasies, outfitted in burgundy surgical gowns, black rubber aprons and gloves. The procedures are nauseatingly gruesome, performed with garden implements, medical instruments, common house tools. The twist: where purveyors of dark tourism typically pay to observe or occupy a space, "hunters" pay to inflict suffering.

Mid-summer on break from college, my sister, a few friends, and I drove through the Village of Camillus one evening. We passed a flower shop, the old cutlery factory, a gas station and ice cream shop, small library, tavern. We drove out past our old middle school off Route 5, its corners and roofline cut against the sky. I shuffled directions, routed and printed from MapBlast before we piled into the car, giddy and nervous, headed for Whiskey Hollow.

We drove around Baldwinsville, looking for the road that would take us to the haunted stretch. We'd gleaned different stories from the Internet. They started to blur together—what we read, what we were told: a bloody blanket in a tree, Satanic cults, someone awaiting execution kept in a house at one end of the road and mysteriously dying by the time someone came for them. The night was humid. We kept seeing distant lightning.

We found the road. It looked like the lightning had been striking where we turned. Like we'd seen it as a beacon, but this may be what I wanted to believe. We drove a dark, narrow length—no streetlights or homes, dense trees on both sides. At the end, we turned to head home. Someone said if we were brave we'd go back and drive it again, slower this time.

We backtracked and someone dared whoever was driving to stop. My chest tightened. I wouldn't look out at all the dark around us. A friend rolled down her window. She stuck her hand out like it was nothing and it was, but I asked her to roll up the window. No one got out. The shine from the headlights was worse than the dark, illuminating what could have been in the trees.

*

Morbid Anatomy closes in mid-December 2016. Unceremonious and abrupt—social media posts, followers lamenting, a *New York Times* write-up like an obituary. The museum, and the response to its closure, highlighted a community interest in what the founders described as *the interstices of art and medicine, death and culture*.[7]

A shed reindeer antler with a bottle opener on one end hangs on a kitchen hook. Apothecary-jarred candles decorate our shelves. As reminders of cycles—life and death, sick and well—these trinkets are subtler than the spectacular gilded and bejeweled taxidermy pieces by Les Deux Garçons, or Kate Clark's hauntingly expressive centaur-esque creations.

The Greek *taxis* means arrangement and *derma* means skin. An arrangement of skin that represents an intersection of art, natural history, and biology.

Taxidermy may be commercially consumed—framed insects, mounted antlers, balsa wood mounts shaped like animal heads; relegated to kitsch, like the works displayed on the website crappytaxidermy.com, which memorializes unsuccessful attempts at preservation—an archive of frayed fur, oddly placed eyes, awkward postures, unnatural facial expressions; regarded as art worthy of fellowships and exhibitions. Such is the case with rogue taxidermy, *a genre of pop-surrealist art characterized by mixed-media sculptures containing traditional taxidermy materials used in an unconventional manner.*[8] A winged monkey clutching a martini glass. A deer's slim frame the diorama of a haunted house, the sides cut out to reveal small rooms like domestic organs inside the animal. A plush toy dog's forehead adorned with a silver horn.

The short story "Congress" by Joy Williams follows a woman traveling with her lover, a professor. Accompanying them, a student and the taxidermy lamp he gifts the professor. Miriam bonds with the lamp, conversing with it so deeply the lamp seems to sense her inner weather. The car stalls out in a rural town. The trio takes to a hotel near a taxidermy museum with an all-knowing taxidermist who appears in a window to demonstrate and answer questions about his process. A man and his child observe a polar bear display alongside Miriam. The three make a trinity: optimistic pretending, deadpan realism, and naïve belief.

"She's protecting her newborn cubs, that's why she's snarling like that," the man said.
"It's dead," Miriam remarked. "The whole little family."
"Hi, polar bear," the child crooned. "Hi, hi, hi."
"What's the matter with you?" the father demanded of Miriam. "People like you make me sick."[9]

Biology in taxidermy observes behavior, expressions, physiology, and death. Natural history pinpoints habitats where specimens are displayed and their place on the evolutionary timeline.

Darkness is acceptable and even attractive so long as there is a threshold that is not crossed.[10]

*

High school summer vacation one year, I stayed up at night before the computer my mother, sister, and I shared. I pored over lyrics about broken hearts, poison, and traffic lights. Songs about dying and car wrecks, night and love. Friends and I instant messaged—neon pink, aqua blue, and red thoughts floating on black backgrounds. Browser windows indexed serial killers, haunted places in Upstate New York, friends' online journals.

Hunkered down in a living room with snacks and drinks, a fan blowing on us to ease the July heat. We watch one episode after another—two men, each laden with their own wrongs against selves and loved ones, try to unravel the source of ritualized deaths as they traverse bayous and forests, abandoned buildings and unkempt greenery.

Home on break during grad school a different summer, my sister mentioned a TV show of staged reenactments detailing supposedly real freak accidents, most of which echoed the symbolic retribution etched in *Se7en*, or the more recent *Saw* films. Men who snorted fire ants, for example, died of bites to their nasal membranes and throats.

My friends and I watched *Saw* at a sleepover in high school. We watched it again and again like it was *Real World* reruns, like it was Tiffani Thiessen or Candace Cameron on Lifetime, like it was Kate Hudson playing a '70s music groupie or Rachel Leigh Cook playing an artist-turned-prom-queen. It was background to AIM chats, painting our nails, flat-ironing our hair, even if we were staying in for the night.

Dave and I sink into the gold upholstery of our living room couch, taking the serial killer series two episodes a night until we have no episodes left to watch.

Two heavy notes from the television speakers. My mother on the couch, working a quarter across a ribbon of scratch-off tickets. TV marathons of dying and investigations. The screen awash in blues and grays. Two notes followed by the whining theme song.

The looming difference is in the name: true crime. It's real, or based on actual events, or based on a story based on actual events.

At the end of the detective show's season finale, one detective says to the other: *Well, once, there was only dark. If you ask me, the light's winning.*[11]

*

Bold blue FWD, an unread chain letter sailed into an inbox. Myspace messages or bulletin posts among surveys answered to kill time: last song you listened to, last time you cried, favorite colors, zodiac sign, relationship status, first surgery. Chain letters said something extremely fortunate or terrible would happen to the reader, depending on whether they reposted or forwarded the message: a wish could come true, a crush could call at midnight to declare undying devotion. A spirit—usually a child, probably with glowing eyes or a bloody face—would show up at midnight and disembowel the reader, gouge out their eyes. Everything always happens at midnight in chain letters and, often, very unfortunate things happen to eyes.

We forwarded the messages, even though we knew the stories were untrue. They cast the same chill I'd felt reading R. L. Stine's *Goosebumps* and Alvin Schwartz's *Scary Stories to Tell in the Dark*, watching *Are You Afraid of the Dark?*. Chain letters were their own genre, which may have been an early form of creepypasta, short horror stories repeatedly shared online, across websites and forums. The term *creepypasta* is a botch on *copypasta*, a mangle of *copy-paste*. Subjects of the letters included an unlucky babysitter, slumber party attendees, a ghost boy with empty eye sockets pouring blood. My friends and I were superstitious enough to believe sharing these stories would secure us deeply lucky futures or save us from terrible fates.

An illustrator details a haunting in his apartment, a ghost he calls Dear David. He documents the events unfolding in a Twitter thread. He peppers in photos and videos—a chair moving, his cat meowing at the front door, a boy's blurry deformed face. Each thread elicits concern from followers, recommendations to move. People tag friends to share the story.

A chain letter, a shared book, watching with other scared people. Fragments threaded into story. Like school bus chatter bouncing between green rubber seats. *Did you hear about* before something awful is shared, the thrill of enrapturing an audience.

My father brought my sister and me along on a business trip to Alexandria Bay. We went out to dinner at a waterfront restaurant. As the hostess led us to our table on the dock, I thought the restaurant was fancy, even though the menus were printed on paper placemats and I ended up ordering a cheeseburger. I looked out at the St. Lawrence River, the water lapping the dock. I swore I saw two eyes staring up at me, two eyes glowing beside a rock. I didn't think my father would believe me if I said anything. I told myself it was trash, crushed aluminum foil, two pearls. I tried to focus on something else, but I could not stop looking at the water, those eyes.

College students head for a weekend at an isolated cabin and awaken a *zombie redneck torture family*[12] after reading a diary found in the cellar. The students are pawns in an operation that mandates an annual blood sacrifice to gods who will wipe out humanity if not appeased. Scientists engineer every aspect of the trip. Atomized pheromones, orchestrated lighting, a high-tech underground facility moderates the environment and the students' behavior to align with horror tropes and archetypes— the whore, the scholar, the athlete, the fool, the virgin. "The whore" bleaches her hair blond before the trip, makes out with a taxidermy wolf on a dare. "The fool" is constantly stoned, his lines spoken in a hazy drawl. Even the cabin setting is recognizable. It's entertaining to watch the characters live out our expectations for them in a place the genre has told us, again and again, to fear.

The precedent embeds humor within the horror. An uneasy laugh almost eases the fear. See *Friday the 13th*, *Sleepaway Camp*, *Evil Dead*, plus all their sequels and remakes. See *Cabin Fever* or *Dreamcatcher*. A virus in the water rots people alive in a cabin. A haunted spellbook found in a basement awakens zombies or spirits, inspires possession: *Someone's in my fruit cellar. Someone with a fresh soul.*[13]

The characters are amplified familiars—someone I know, someone I have met before. They're family or friends, or friends of friends, or my own self.

College students renting the apartment behind my house hang out on their patio. They talk about spring break abroad. At a club on the last night, a guy hangs all over a group of friends. One friend makes out with the guy. He invites her back to his place, but she's heading home the next day so she declines. A few days after arriving home, a rash flowers around her mouth. She goes to the doctor, who asks if she has been eating humans because she has a bacterial disease only present in rotting human flesh. She tells the doctor about her last night abroad. The doctor links the woman's hook-up to a news story about a man who was recently arrested for murder. The police found at least one, possibly several, partially consumed bodies in his flat.

A hand may flutter to a chest in a contained swoon. Someone on the patio may tell someone else who may tell someone else. Almost anyone who hears this story knows it's not true. Maybe they've heard it before, perhaps with some variation. The setting was Miami, not Prague. The rash was viral, not bacterial. Or there was no rash at all and the woman woke with maggots crawling from her mouth.

We've heard this one before. We know better. We're versed in urban legends. We know the ending. We listen because the story satisfies an urge toward darkness and promises relief: we are not in the story.

14.

Brief phrases and single words exist to describe complex, specific feelings. The French *l'espirit d'escalier*—the spirit of the stairs, thinking of the right thing to say after it's called for, the comeback or response like a ghost on a staircase, missed any time someone tries to see it. *L'appel du vide*—the call of the void, the sudden desire to jump from a bridge while standing on it, the impulse to swerve into oncoming traffic.

I love the gentle ways to speak of dying; elegant phrasing softens the sudden drop and vastness: passing on, no longer of this earthly plane, *shuffle off this mortal coil*. And inhabit what?

Since the 1950s, hundreds of dogs in Dumbarton, Scotland, have leapt from the Overtoun Bridge. Science says the dogs jump because they are drawn to animal scents in the gorge. Superstition says the bridge is a *"thin place," a mesmerizing spot where heaven and earth overlap.*[1] Like the stones below are a veil between the living and the dead.

I won't cross a bridge if I can avoid it, especially on foot. The last time I did, I ran across, headed toward a pizza shop with a large group of friends to celebrate a birthday.

L'appel du vide provokes a physical reaction—adrenaline release, quickened heart rate. Some researchers note it represents a core desire to live. Others suggest these thoughts reflect an increased risk of suicide. I want to know what's most horrifically thrilling about a near-death experience: the event itself or describing it later; the saying or the listener's reaction. Or is it the sense of almost: hearing the void's call and refusing to answer.

*

I opened the filter, index finger in the hole to lift the cover from the deck. I emptied the basket on the lawn and replaced it. I startled at the garter snake circling the filter, my hand so close to the snake's body flush against the caulk, snug inside a groove.

I put my hand in water where I could not see bottom. I took off my shoes and socks, swirled my feet. I put my finger in the recessed space of a television's power button and got zapped. I died more than once one night in my dreams. Instead of running from the cave, I walked into the darkness, said some words, and listened for what echoed back.

I still have not seen the one with a cover showing six hands pressed flat on frosted glass, bloody handprints smeared across it. A semi-visible face howls through the blur. A pain-moan held up by four other hands. Nor have I seen the one with a woman's back on the cover, scratches on her skin, shoulder blades like wings, a white bodysuit torn off one shoulder, smeared in dirt and blood, some hair sweat-stuck to the back of her neck, shoulders pulled back, a defiant posture. One hand grips a bloody knife. Her other fist holds nothing or hides something we can't see.

I used to avoid looking. Or I looked in a distracted way because one time what I saw ruffled my middle like fabric caught beneath a sewing needle. A man and woman fought on the living room television. I was eating a grilled ham sandwich with mustard, seated at the yellow and red plastic table. Shouting rose on the speakers. The characters' bodies tangled. My heart dashed hard in my chest, my middle coiled, my hunger left me. A friend of my mother's was watching me at her house a few days later. I sat at the kitchen table as she prepared my lunch. I asked for the sandwich cold; the thought of toasted bread and hot mustard reminded me of bones and voices thudding against walls and floors.

Always some other noise around me; a radio, a record player, a TV show or movie, a singalong with a bouncing ball and a chorus of birds.

My brother and father were watching a movie on the living room television. I listened when I should have been tuning out. I sat on the gold carpeting, carefully arranging animals in the Littlest Pet Shop, securing Polly Pocket in a clamshell beauty parlor, half-focused on the screen. The cursing and music indicated I should not see this movie, but I kept glancing. My parents fought when my mother saw I was there, I was watching. My father turned it off or I left the room. I don't remember, but I still haven't seen this movie.

*

Sometimes the unseen is more terrifying than what's in view. Movie magic, special effects. Like a shower scene that does not actually show the knife plunged into or pulled from a victim's flesh. Absence—of light, safety, details—is horror. Blankness is horror. What the imagination adds to the blank space; how it answers the open-ended questions.

A final girl gets longer. She does not know how much. There could be a sequel, or several, plus spinoffs. She may be a cautionary tale or joke. She could be a legend, immortalized and called back, time and again, through reverent homage, parody, or reboot.

*

He showed up daily for two weeks, standing at the desk and forcing conversation. He clutched a backpack to his chest and stared at me as he spoke. I clicked at the keyboard, updating store inventory, replying to emails, or writing drafts to no one to appear busy. He stepped closer to the desk one afternoon, *I want to ask you something because you are nice.* I stood slowly, prepared to call for my coworker. I met his gaze, enough to see what was happening, but not enough to count as eye contact. I felt heavy and afraid waiting for whatever he had to say. *I want to ask if you'll be my spiritual guide.*

Sleeping over at my friend's house, we heard howls cut the night air. I hardly slept, the soft sheets suddenly irritating my skin. I thought if I went onto the balcony, I'd see coyotes on the ground. They sounded so close. I pulled the covers to my neck, imagined the coyotes impatient with our resting. I saw them flying up from the ground, looking in the window, eyes aglow.

*

I waited for a ride in a bus shelter beside a guardless kiosk. I thought of the cemetery around the corner. Dog song filled the night, howls and yips from a direction I couldn't distinguish. I called my sister. She said she was a few minutes away. Time distended, I panicked, wondering whether coyotes were like objects seen in side mirrors—closer than they sound. I thought of the animated movie where a woman leaves a castle and rides into a blizzard and wolves circle her in the woods. I saw no shapes between the trees, no glowing eyes among the branches and bushes. My sister's car swung into the lot. I ran for the passenger door.

Coyote attacks on humans are rare. Had I known I wasn't in danger, I'd have been no less afraid; I have yet to find a harmonious coexistence between logic and panic.

Six years later at a party, sitting around a bonfire, I heard it again—dog chorus, wild and loud.

...then you hear that terrible high-pitched screaming. The ocean turns red, and despite all the pounding and the hollering they all come in, they rip you to pieces.[2]

One friend promised the coyotes sounded close, but were far away. Another said that's how they greet each other. Someone else said the calls meant they'd found something they liked, which I took to mean they were tearing an animal apart. An image flickered before me—wild dogs circling all of us, pacing between the trees as they licked their mouths, silent until they attacked. I went inside the house and would not go back outside, even after the calls stopped.

Running is not advised during a wild animal encounter. A more successful strategy for evading attack is hazing, as in: *To haze is to scare the animal away from you.*

The university Greek system prohibits hazing, or: *Force (a new or potential recruit to the military or a university fraternity) to perform strenuous, humiliating, or dangerous tasks.*

I know someone who dropped out of pledging during Hell Week when his future "brothers" covered their basement floor in rainbow sprinkles before some sorority pledges. The ex-pledge told me the women pledges were given instructions to sort the sprinkles by color as fraternity brothers emptied bottles of chocolate syrup on the sprinkles and pledges.

To haze a coyote, the advice is: *Make yourself look as big, imposing, and aggressive as possible.*[3]

Hazing in another context may mean: *Drive (cattle) while on horseback.*

My second year of college, up late, writing papers or reading, I took cigarette breaks outside the dorm where I lived. A week during February, like migrating flocks, women left the building in long puffy jackets, adjusting hats and pulling on gloves as they trudged through knee-high snow in negative windchills. The drifts moved into the night, toward sorority row. *Hell Week* a friend called it, but she wouldn't tell me more than that. I worried for her and other friends I knew pledging. I'd seen movies, heard stories. For all I knew though, the things I imagined happening were replaced by movie nights, songs about sisterhood. What I didn't know—and what I filled that unknowing with—may have been more horrifying.

*

We go to the Adirondacks, a cabin belonging to an inn. We hike the trails on the property. The air has a water-clean freshness to it, a sweet stinging perfume of green needles. Tiny pinecones decorate the dirt.

We descend a hill and see a horse farm. The path winds along a fence, leads to more hilly woods. We reach a pond and sit on a fallen tree, the wood dark and damp. The cracked parts reveal sapwood and heartwood shredded like barbecue meat, the rings indiscernible so we can't know how old the tree was when it died.

The pond is peaceful, some trees gold or red, in the peak of brilliant change. I inhale deeply, look around, feeling the air filling me. On a nearby bank, among tree trunks, I catch a moving black shape. I think the shape is a bear, but it could be a shadow. Dave says to stay calm and he tries to look. He films a video on his phone. Neither of us knows for sure what we see.

We hike back to our cabin. I'm almost running. My legs make their own momentum. Dave says not to run, in case the shadow is a bear. He says *Stop* and *You have to listen*. Serious as ever, he says, *If there really is a bear you can't run because you're going to get us both killed if you do.* But it's like I don't hear him or my fear doesn't care; I talk loudly, breathe shallow and fast. I pull the map to our cabin from the pocket of my denim jacket. It seems pointless to try outrunning a bear. I can't stop thinking, *The bear is faster. The bear will catch up.*

The hour hike to the pond is a twenty-minute clip back. I jump at each snapping branch, every not-human footprint, the leaves fifteen feet away rustling before a single wild turkey crosses the path ahead of us. I feel terrified to be outdoors, surrounded by trees, all the ongoing outside. I feel suddenly very aware how easily we could become part of the landscape. The gold, red, and orange I admired hiking to the pond becomes a burning quilt above us, a fiery canopy.

Afraid while watching a monster movie, a cartoon character closes his eyes and then anguishes the rest of the episode over the monster he missed. He has nightmares about what he didn't see: a red skyline, buildings with eyes, a traffic light walks the street on long cable legs, saying: *You know the scariest thing about me, kid. You don't even know what I look like.*[4] Returning to the movie a third time, the character commits to keeping his eyes opened during the reveal. The monster isn't as horrifying as he expected; the costume zipper up the monster's back is visible.

*

My uncle's brusque voice played back on the answering machine years ago. Recuperating from back surgery, he'd called to tell my mother about his recovery. Rather than wait for her to call back, he left a long message with all the details. He and my aunt used to send annual Christmas cards reviewing the year about to end—their garden yield, vacations, hunting trips.

Dave and I are drinking beer and eating happy-hour fries at a bar after work. I glance at my phone, see a missed call from my mother. I call her back and she answers when I'm almost home, reaching for the mailbox. She asks if I am sitting down. I say I'm not but it's okay. She tells me her brother took his life. She catalogues the family's suicides. She punctuates each with what she says is the reason each person made this choice. The why seems more fraught than any explanation she offers, but how would either of us know.

Counting change the next day at work, I'm distracted replaying what I was told. Sharp blur of images I can't stop seeing. His voice on the message machine years before. I ask to leave work early. I say my uncle *passed away*. The phrase *passed away* sounds too gentle for what happened.

*

I wake and care for the pets the morning after my father-in-law ends his life. I walk our dog, shroud her pills in lunchmeat so she'll swallow them, feed her and our cats. Dave has flown to South Carolina to be with his family. I don't know what to do with myself. Feeding the pets is a thermometer to measure what I need. I try writing. I cry and listen to music. I take a shower to get ready for work and wobble in the water. I feel weak and heavy, outside myself, like nothing is happening as my body yields to some unseen major impact. I take the day off to be by myself and sit in the sunroom at the back of our apartment. I sew café curtains for the window in the door, which looks onto the funeral home across the street.

A friend takes me to Wegmans. We sit in her car and the purple-gray sky mists. I say, *It's so messed up* over and over. I say, *I can't*, but I don't know what I'm saying I can't do. I can't believe it. I can't talk about it or understand it. I can't bring him back.

It is rare to hear someone died by suicide and not know how they did it, and even more rare to hear someone died from complications relating to mental illness. The unveiling of method is so common following a suicide it seems expected. If a newspaper reports on a suicide and includes the method, a cascade effect occurs. Additional papers will likely include the same information, though they may ultimately publish a different story.

The next day I go to work. My boss says he read about it in the paper, how sorry he is. A South Carolina newspaper published the details, location and method. Other papers, including the local Ithaca paper, ran versions that acknowledged these facts. A man who used to come through my co-op line to buy the daily paper—where my husband was a reporter when we first moved to Ithaca—passes where I work. He notices me at the desk and comes in, saying, *I saw the paper* and *I'm sorry* and *It's no one's fault* even though all I say is *Hello*. I'm too stunned to respond. He keeps talking until I say, *Thank you*. I'm not sure my gratitude is real. I don't know him well enough to talk about it. I fix my eyes on the small statue of Don Quixote on the desk and think of all the people who have asked to buy it. I focus on the silvery hat brim, the ridges in his armor.

*

I researched hiking spots before Dave and I went to the Adirondacks, fixated on timber rattlesnakes. I found internet forums for tourists and nature enthusiasts. Making our itinerary, I excluded places with reviews mentioning rattlesnakes. I mapped directions from our cabin to rattlesnake spottings. I wanted us to be safe. I studied maps highlighting snake territory, calculated their proximity to our cabin and tried to guess how far snakes travel in their lifetimes. I read how to handle a rattlesnake encounter when I could have started with something simple, like how to identify a rattlesnake. I could have learned what to look for instead of considering bells tied on shoelaces, hiking with a stick to tap while walking, vibrating the earth to alert snakes. I didn't think of bears. I focused on the ground where we stepped as we walked the trails. My eyes laser-focused on leaf piles and stones. Any place a snake could hide. I listened for a rattle. I wanted to keep us safe.

15.

Dave and I backed out of the driveway of an enormous blue beach house, preparing to drive home from the Outer Banks to Ithaca. We rolled down the windows to say, *Goodbye*, which we thought was really, *So long*.

I have tried replacing *goodbye* with *so long*. It's what I mean—*It will feel like so long until we see each other again*. *Goodbye* is steeped in finality.

Our dog paced the back seat. We put our hands out the windows to wave.

*

An orbit, as I have known it. A ring, a retrograde. The feeling goes away and comes back, sinks and resurfaces. A retrograde hangover, or *retroshade*. I have yet to see a straight line through grief. Like a ghost whose outline eludes me; a movie I have seen and watch again.

Several times a year from Earth, Mercury appears to reverse its orbit. Astrology says the planet rules communications, so a retrograde period suggests botched correspondence, delayed flights, chaos hurling itself at organizational endeavors, abandoned plans. Depending on a person's superstitions, planning a trip or signing a contract is ill-advised during Mercury retrograde.

The word *catharsis* implies release. How I feel pulses—tightens and relaxes. I try assuring myself something happening at the moment will not happen forever.

Mercury does not move backward during retrograde. That's only how it looks.

*

Each grief-wake is shaped differently, the patterns and effects like watercraft on the ocean—dependent on craft speed, water depth, whether the water was already disturbed. I feel helpless knowing someone who has died will never stop being dead. The world asks nothing else of them, while I keep up with life's momentum, gracefully carry their end and ongoing absence.

Our tasks dovetail; their being dead and my being alive, two enduring constants.

Whether it came slowly, an illness progressed, or unexpectedly, death has bent sunsets, coiled the horizon into a shining lariat I sometimes forget I am wearing. I move a certain way and feel the metal against my chest, surprising and cold, even though it's familiar. Or the chain twists uncomfortably and I put both hands to my neck, unwind the links. I feel it in how I love, how I care for myself and people around me, how quiet sounds, how I speak.

If I press play on a *Texas Chainsaw Massacre* movie, I know it's coming: quiet like a snowstorm. The moment when a fleeing character stops and listens for footsteps, rustling leaves, tree branches cracking in half, a door or floorboard creaking. I like the bone-deep silence before the engine revs and the chain whines and Leatherface emerges steering the blade. And I still jump.

*

My face, too, lives up to the feeling. My reflection shows me as much as old photos—softer cheeks, lighter eyes, a face less carved by the sharp corners that caught it. I reassure myself another year will soften the edges.

*

A shade pulled over a window, a room darkening and cooling. Hopelessness complicates healing. I missed it more than once, but that is the before, a place of preparation, and I am thinking of the after because that's where I live. Steel-drum stretches, empty and hollow. My ears ring with loud quiet so intricately sad and isolating it sounds like metal hitting metal.

Time pulls thick, opaque as taffy. I can't see to the other side. I get stuck in it.

*

Dave drives to New Jersey to spend the anniversary of his father's death with his mother. An enormous snowstorm hits the East Coast. I spend the week writing and cleaning the house, shoveling every few hours so the accumulation will not weigh more than I can lift. The yellow handle breaks off the shovel. It's the brightest object on the street.

I go to therapy. I go to a tattoo shop and make an appointment. Dave calls each night. I say how much snow fell, that my arms and back feel tired and sore. A friend and I see a movie about street cats in Istanbul. Each featured cat is named for their personality. The cats, delightful music, and compassion of the people who care for the cats lifts the heaviness pulling the week along. All the people interviewed remark on a similar feeling— a sense of responsibility to the animals. I want the house immaculate by the time Dave returns, the sidewalk and driveway clear, as if the storm never happened. A black sedan parked across the street is still buried to the tops of its tires.

Lucie Brock-Broido's poem "Dire Wolf" is sedimentary, layering love and grief, which may feel boundless, but are often hemmed in by certain parameters: *There//Are things which can dismantle entirely/A spirit, such as the pathetic maledictive fear// Of loss. Of loss:/You get to speak of it, once//You are its intimate, and not before; it would be/"Appropriation." But in the great white rendezvous, where//I was brooding/Just a while, you get to speak of dire love.*[1]

Bracing for loss by fearing it offers no relief. It may even be its own kind of dying.

*

Watching zombie movies with other people usually inspires a chain reaction of plan sharing. Each person lays out where they would go, survival partners, weapons. My plan: I would stay in my house with a nailed board and invite over all my friends to eat and get drunk. The likely unfolding: I would run into the street instead of waiting to die alone.

It's cool to have a zombie apocalypse plan but morbid to think of one's own funeral. It's the difference between a survivalist fantasy and dismal certainty.

·A friend and I talk about our current reads. I mention Caitlin Doughty's *Smoke Gets in Your Eyes*, which chronicles the author's path to becoming a mortician and comments on United States death culture. The person flinches at the description, the mention of death. I worry I've said something impolite.

Someone sent the following to the etymology website Grammarphobia: *...I'd often assumed an "undertaker" was called that because he took someone under the ground. But on reflection, I wonder if it comes from the fact that he undertakes something we don't want to talk about.* Writers and editors Patricia T. O'Conner and Stewart Kellerman confirm the word means *someone who undertakes a task.* The moniker *has been used to mean a businessman, a writer, a lobbyist, a contractor, a tax collector, a scholar, and an impresario, among others.*[2]

Passing funeral homes, I wonder about the consistently perfect landscaping, whether it's standard among them to keep shrubs and lawns impeccably groomed. Neat, safe, ordered, healthy. The family that owns the funeral home near my house also owns the local ambulance, two houses separated by a driveway and parking lot. Everyone makes the same joke about it.

Workbook-style pages of funeral preparation questions follow John Troyer's lecture, "On the Non-Denial Denial of Death" in *The Morbid Anatomy Anthology. What I would most like my family and friends to understand about my life, what was important to me, and what I learned from life are described below. The last thing I would like to say is.*[3] Planning gives the dead a last way to say farewell. It also carves space for sorrow and remembering; the bereaved may carry out arrangements and mourn, rather than making plans.

Everyone has a death, but some people don't want to talk or hear about it; they don't want to think about theirs. My mother mentioned an upcoming trip to see her sister, who suggested they visit their parents in the cemetery. My mother called this morbid. She has said she wants to die in her sleep. She wants medicine to make it happen when it's time. Death seems to her the ultimate unendurable violence. I have not asked how she feels about all that happens before.

*

Stepping into the funeral home for my father's mother's wake, the space reminded me of a dentist's office and a church—clean, professional, and sacred. Above the door to the salon where my grandmother lay for viewing, a black nameplate stamped with her name in thin white letters. I was named for this grandmother, so seeing the nameplate felt like being inside a sad, calm nightmare. The letters like bones in the dark. I felt sinking recognition, like when a tech flips the illuminator switch—my bones aglow on X-ray film.

Years before, wearing plastic ruby slippers and a white leotard swirled with glittering stars, I traipsed the hallway from the living room to the den. The shoes clicked with each step. My eyes focused on the purple and green slate floor tiles. I played funeral, pricked my finger on a barbell peg and stretched out on the padded weightlifting bench. I called my family to mourn me. I took it all so seriously. It was my death, after all.

*

Scattered anniversaries. Inventory of after. All the missing and sadness. All I can't see happening inside my body. A new way people see me. A new way I see myself, knowing I am a limb on this family tree; blood and brain grown from the same roots.

I want to say a shift in grieving a suicide is to stop asking why, but I haven't stopped yet. I don't know how; or it's a question whose true answer might hurt too much to learn. It's painful to think too long about a family member whose intense suffering eclipses the promise of another option. It's frightening to recognize I can feel such enormous pain and the potential to make the same choice.

I ask, *Why not me?* I don't know. I know a person preparing to end her life may seem buoyant, as if preparing to go on vacation, or she appears to have *turned a corner*. A person on the cusp of a birthday is more likely to die, it's called the birthday effect; specifically, the birthday blues and suicide are linked to comparing past years and the one about to end, especially if previous years were filled with more success or happiness. Uncertainty over whether another successful, happy year will ever happen again can induce a tailspin. I don't know what, if anything, divides me from family members who have attempted and family members who have died by suicide. I don't like hearing suicide described in terms of failure or success. I don't know if thinking about any of this makes me any more or less likely to end my life.

Taking care of myself is not as exhausting as worrying about it. A checklist of sleep, eat, and exercise habits. Am I taking vitamins, dressing, and making my appointments? Should I eat less sugar, more greens and avocados? Is any of this working?

*

A new set of mirrors reflects back into infinity. Someone asks no questions and I assume they feel uncomfortable talking about it. Someone asks questions and I clam up or brace with worry, anticipating judgement. On occasion, whoever I'm talking with flinches. Without thinking of their own struggle, their own experiences, I worry they think something must be wrong with me or my family.

I worry despair is contagious and if I'm not careful I'll infect everyone around me.

In a horror movie, an infected character may hide a bite or rash, an urge, an unwellness. She might withdraw or act out, or behave as if nothing is the matter, nothing has happened. Any course of action opposite saying how she feels suggests suffering privately is preferable to the anticipated betrayal of being cast out.

I am fogged with constant sadness and fear that I will grieve other people who take their own lives. Someone jokes, *I'd kill myself.* I want to ask, *Would you really?*

The voicemail message my mother left me on the day my uncle died is still in my inbox: *This isn't an emergency, but I need to talk to you about something.* I visualize a ticker tape getting stuck in my head, a feeling jamming up. A calm, wide, confident cloud. This isn't an emergency until it is, or until the emergency is over.

16.

I walk along Cascadilla Gorge. The steep staircase beneath the College Avenue Stone Arch Bridge. People take pictures beside the falls. They put their arms around each other on stone benches. They smile. If I stand too close to the edge, my heart surges and my stomach churns; a sad ache falls through me. I don't go up any further. I take a picture of myself with the waterfall behind me. I sit and look up at the bridge, a net stretched from under each side of the deck.

In Toronto, the Prince Edward Viaduct's suicide barrier is called the Luminous Veil. The name conjures *beyond the veil*—a state of unknowns and uncertainty, a mysterious place, like what happens when we die—and transforms it to light, a purple-blue glow coming on at night.

The nets here don't have names. Walking down the gorge, I look up at the Stewart Avenue Bridge. I hadn't noticed the nets on my climb, only the bridge, how high it is, the rock layers extending to the deck. Some rocks are wet. Water trickles from an unknown source.

*

My mother gave me a goldenrod mailer lined in deflated green bubble wrap. Clippings and dance programs fill the envelope.

Performance stills of my great uncle leaping mid-air, school photos, summer workshop snapshots, letters he wrote backstage, reviews and announcements for ballets he danced, his *Dance Magazine* cover issue, an old issue of *Time* with a brief write-up and black-and-white photo of him bending his torso as Adam around Eve in *Original Sin*.

The clippings and photos highlight my great uncle's absence, the gorge cracked open. Leafing through feels like filling a flower-bed with water and watching the soil slowly absorb the puddle.

Among the ephemera, a letter from *Dance Magazine* columnist Russell Hartley to my great uncle's mother. Hartley shares that he and a friend scattered my great uncle's ashes at Mount Tamalpais and ...*the only observers were two deer and a squirrel.*

I think of photos of mountain ranges and rainbows, rivers, oceans, canyons; an optimistic quote below an impossible-looking landscape. I want my sadness and survival to be specific to my experiences. How sincere to my strength is the same ocean and quote someone else attaches to their strength? Am I selfish for asking? What if I asked instead: why did I choose an ocean? Why did I talk about it? Is aversion to sharing urged by the mechanism that stirs a flinch at the mention of death, of suicide?

In her lecture "On Sentimentality," Mary Ruefle writes: *We are human beings. Our expressions are always inadequate, often pitiful... All we can say in defense of our insane tribulations is that they were an act of love—a supremely sentimental act—an act of causeless emotion—that made us commit embarrassing gestures.*[1]

One *embarrassing gesture* I'm guilty of is not asking who else might choose an ocean; what kind would they pick? What does the water mean to them?

I take inventory of objects around me to calm myself. To record takes on new vitality. I focus on parts working together to keep life happening. Moss, dirt, pollen, water, thick bees with dense fur and humming wings. Sometimes I forget the sun.

From these views remains the possibility of night coming on inside me. I practice remaining present. The smooth feel of my desk; light falling in a room to throw a pretty shadow on a wall; pulling the bed linens up to my neck, making a cocoon as I fall asleep. The soft texture at the back of Dave's neck, below the hairline, how he smells in the morning—deodorant and sleep's clean sweat. The lilts when he speaks, his voice a soft boom in my ear.

*

I'm trying to stare down despair and tell it, *I have lived with you for many years and I plan to live alongside you for many more.* My mistake is neither in permitting, nor dwelling. The tripwire is saying—secretly believing and hoping—*I'll never feel that way again.*

Survival may have less to do with strength and bravery and more to do with tenderness and vulnerability. Asking *How long can I sit here with this feeling?*

The spot beneath my chest that swells with compassion is the same place I feel the ache. If an experiment were to induce how I feel when I kiss and when I panic and project these sensations on a screen, the graphics would look similar, a plunge. I try to tell myself *Stop* or *This feels painful* when I feel myself start to slip. I try to name where in my body the feeling lives.

Adrenaline and *l'appel du vide*. A road and an oncoming car. A bridge with water rushing far beneath it. Wanting to die and live at the same time. Wanting to talk without burdening anyone.

An optometrist shines a light in my eye. He swings the mask with sight inside it down on its long arm. He swivels corrective lenses before my eyes and asks, *Better? Or worse? One or two? Two or three?* He toggles back and forth until I make up my mind, which view is clearest.

*

I climb stone stairs to the cemetery, an overlook where bright green moss grows in corners and masonry seams. A view of the city. A view to the lake. The top of a tomb is visible. Off the path, down a slight incline—a brick wall, a stone slab, a plaque engraved with a name: Wait.

Distrust everything if you have to./But trust the hours. Haven't they/carried you everywhere, up to now? Galway Kinnell's poem "Wait" continues: *Don't go too early./You're tired. But everyone's tired./But no one is tired enough.*[2]

I worked at a bookstore that sold used paperbacks and hardcovers alongside rare finds. I wandered during lulls, filled shelf gaps, checked alphabetization. I read passages and admired plates. Animals in Thomas Bewick's *A General History of Quadrupeds*. Green cloth-bound volumes in publisher William Wood's medical and surgical monographs series—*Diseases of Women, Handbook of Electro-Therapeutics*. A small, rare hardcover published by Tiffany and Co.—*Natal Stones*—described jewelry trends throughout history. I liked the acrostic rings. Designed to express sentiment, the first letter of each stone spelled out a message or term of endearment—*Adore, Regard, Dearest*. A for amethyst, D for diamond, O for opal.

Someone special-ordered a book about diatoms, microorganisms that leave behind shells when they die. The shells are the abrasive particles in toothpaste. I used to feel more grossed out brushing my teeth with the skeleton of something once alive.

While working in the garden, my father would sometimes riff off the ironic final twist of a horror anthology episode. He used to tell my sister and me: *The good news is we removed the bug. The bad news is it was a female and it laid hundreds of eggs.* My sister and I chopped locust skeletons with sticks in the driveway one evening. A shell split and out came earwigs. My sister wore a fleece winter headband over her ears to bed. She did this for weeks.

Gray eyebrows owl-furrowed, my father said earwigs were destroying his garden. He ignited the grill to hear them pop. He said the whistle before the crackling was the insects screaming, though the sound was likely the grill. On another visit he shook a plastic bag of diatomaceous earth and told me the soil would open the earwigs' bellies and their organs would fall out.

My father was different after his father and brother died. The tenor of our conversations changed. Our calls stretched into his reckonings with death, its accumulation, long-term illnesses and split-second keelings. He explained grief, the Kübler-Ross Model, *All That Jazz* and Bob Fosse. He spoke of feeling tired, his gray hair. Our talks zigzagged like helium balloons someone filled up and let go in a high-ceilinged room.

Close a door to a room. Give away the objects left. Shred the papers. The want to clutch any reminder versus the want to keep moving expands and contracts, a pulse.

I try avoiding stasis—days spent staring out the window or at the wall, thinking of all the lives being lived, concentric circles, the impact of lives on lives on lives.

A piano played with the lid propped in an empty room. Slipping into the all-around feel of the noise.

*

My sixth-grade reading class looked at photos of the Titanic covered in ghostly barnacles, the bow where two teenagers flew into a sunset in the movie most of us had seen. The reading focused on history, ship construction, people who carried accounts to a coast. Any light shone in the deep water cast brilliant shades: teal, bright blue, white-hot. We learned about Greek gods and goddesses, myths explaining morals, seasons, and natural disasters. We studied ancient Egypt—pyramids, pharaohs, Nile River silt, canopic jars that vesseled the liver, intestines, stomach, and lungs. The heart was the only organ left in the body. It was believed the heart was weighed in the afterlife and the weight compared to *the feather of truth* to evaluate the person's life. A god with a dog head attended the weighing.

Religions and cultures have long mythologized the psychopomp—a being who guides the dead to the afterlife. In Greek mythology, Charon the ferryman boats the dead to Hades.

Dave gives me a small gold-plated anchor on a long chain. It's stamped *CAPTAIN*. I drive a nail in the blue wall beside where I lay my head. I hang the anchor by its eye.

Grever is an Old French verb meaning to burden and it is one etymological mother of *grief*, descended from Latin's *gravare*, which is to make heavy and descends from *gravis*—evoking weight and heft.

I am not comforted by the idea that someone who dies by suicide is *finally at peace*. Many religions forbid suicide souls from comfortable, or even respectable, afterlives. Some literature depicts suicide souls enduring torture. I know the conversational hiccup and pitying look, someone asking if I knew. *Yes* or *No* seem like the only acceptable answers. Neither one seems exactly correct.

Egyptian myth insisted the heart had to weigh less than the feather of truth for the deceased to enter the afterlife. If a heart was weighed down by sin, it was impossible to enter the afterlife and the person *would cease to exist*.[3]

Friends and I bunched our sleeping bags aside at a sleepover. We made a clearing on the living room floor. One friend stretched flat on her back in the space. Everyone else placed index fingers beneath her and chanted, *Light as a feather, stiff as a board...*

*

An all-encompassing ache. A numb, expansive void. Like being tightened and loosened at the same time. A furniture screw, a slight adjustment determines if the chair will support seated weight or fall apart. A hopeless pang, which sounds how it feels to say—pain, twinge, spasm. A never-quite-full-enough-ness, not always an emptiness. What can feel like a low E on a piano, held for an ongoing time, sustained deep and feeling, almost hopeful. I wait it out. How long can I sit with this feeling until another eclipses it?

My sister said a great-grandmother of ours died by suicide. My sister researched mental health, but called it madness. At my most optimistic, minor research on family history is refusal, a way to say, *I won't.*

Closing a piano lid only reduces the volume a slight amount. The music will still be heard.

*

To conclude our Greek mythology unit, the teacher showed a movie from the '80s. Gods and goddesses move pawns representing mortals on a game board, pitting them against deadly monsters, cruel weather. Always external influences, never double pawns of the same mortal, a person opposing herself.

*

A dice roll's value in tabletop games depends on the game being played and a player's desired outcome. A lower number does not doom a player if the space where they land awards them a generous stack of fake pastel bills. And a higher number doesn't indicate better luck if the space where the player lands sends them to a jail spot or sets off an elaborate contraption that took longer to build than the game lasts.

How many ways may an object be a metaphor; which pawn would I pick? A bridge, a house, a city, a monster, a ghost, a mall, an absence, a gun, a girl, a kiss, a knife, a pill bottle, a lake or ocean, the flower seeds someone told me a person must be eighteen to purchase, a woman crying in a car, a forest, a freezer, a bath. What would it mean to me?

*

A woman settling into her bedroom after arriving at a haunted house notices: *When she stood still in the middle of the room the pressing silence of Hill House came back all around her. I am like a small creature swallowed whole by a monster, she thought, and the monster feels my tiny little movements inside.*[4]

One oversimplified explanation attributes depression to *a chemical imbalance in the brain.* I think of numbers and letters wedged into formulas, translated into smells or pops or fire, clear liquid clouding, turning opaque, cause-and-effect logic.

Are my feelings old feelings? New wood on an old plant blooming fresh, bright pain. Is each sadness a new sadness or a new way to feel sad about the same things? Is *sadness* the right word and how much of it knits with worry and fear? Is my sadness about anything? Must sadness connect to a specific moment or experience for the feeling to matter?

During chemistry labs, I secured safety goggles over my eyes with an elastic band. I mixed indicated amounts and beheld whatever they did. The teacher shut off the lights, the Bunsen burners hissed light in the dim classroom. I clamped small pieces of metal ribbon bathed in compound solutions, extended tongs into fire; the metal made colorful flames whose shades depended on the solution's elemental makeup. Potassium burns a light purple or pinkish flame. Copper streaks blue or green fire. Magnesium burns a sharp, intense white. I remember that a covalent bond between atoms means they share electrons, which have a negative charge.

How much does my heart weigh? How much negative electricity do I carry? What color does each feeling burn?

17.

My breath catches in my throat when Dave says, *We have this whole other life together when we're sleeping.* He means it like a random remark, but it startles me to think we spend half our lives in the same bed, not speaking or interacting, that we know of. We know only so much about what happens when we sleep or die.

*

The premise was familiar before I saw the movie about the man who hurts people in their dreams; cicadas-up-two-octaves music marking a slip from reality into nightmare, a place where the two states meet. When I was younger, a life-size statue of the night-mare man guarded the green-lit horror room at a video store. Poised to swipe a knife glove, his burnt face looked painful and raw. I saw the nightmare man in a TV cartoon—a grounds-keeper terrorizes schoolchildren in their nightmares. I've seen people dressed as the nightmare man on Halloween, the red and green striped sweater, brown fedora, rubber razor gloves.

I've heard what matters isn't what we see in our dreams but how we feel about the images. That each person we see in a dream is a version of ourselves. And someone who falls in a dream and hits the ground will die in real life. That most people's dreams look like black-and-white movies, only some people see colorful dreams. I've heard a variation, everyone sees their dreams in monochrome and some people perceive colors—much like genetic predisposition determines whether someone will like, or dislike, cilantro's soapy herb flavor.

I dream I lift the toilet lid to find a cut-up snake floating in pieces in the bowl. I flush and the head does not go down—the jaw stretched wide, filled with a single egg, floats back to the surface.

The day after her friend is murdered in her bed, a teenager goes to school to stay awake. She struggles to keep her eyes open as her teacher roams the desk aisles, lecturing: *What is seen is not always what is real. According to Shakespeare there was something operating in nature, perhaps inside human nature itself, that was rotten. A canker, as he put it.*[1]

The visitation from a dead parent. A treasure discovery. A fast sprint down a nightmare street to outrun a dangerous form. Falling forever, never nearing the ground. We get jobs or promotions. We tell off bullies or visit dear, old friends as if no time has passed. We bury our faces in the fur of dead pets, miraculously alive again, delighted to see us.

I dream trees grow from dirt mounds on my scalp. The dirt mounds are blemishes. The blemishes are purple-gray mouths, frozen or dead.

Tell a dream, lose a reader, supposedly said Henry James. Maybe a dream only matters to its dreamer. It seems possible to learn more about someone from them telling a dream than from them describing a job, house, or hobby.

Icy music rises. The teenager's eyes fall shut and flicker to a voice whispering her name. She looks into the hall. Her dead friend stands zipped in a body bag, smearing blood on the plastic. A classmate at the front of the room reads in a trance-struck whisper: *O God, I could be bounded in a nutshell, and count myself a king of infinite space, were it not that I have bad dreams.*[2] [3]

A story in the paper when I was a child warned of a rabid raccoon. I thought of a bite, a dirty wound, fever and aches. I read about rabies in a medical encyclopedia. I dreamed I was in the woods and a rabid pig approached, saying it could bite me. I woke up feeling sick and took a bath. I thought of fearing water intensely, a throat seizing as it swallows. I plunked my hands in the water, tried to hold the terror. My fingers wrinkled purple-white.

A bad dream whose symbols are decoded upon waking is still a bad dream.

The teenager tells her parents the killer is still at large after another friend dies. Her parents take her to the hospital for a sleep study. She pulls a fedora hat off the nightmare man's head in a dream. She carries the hat back to waking life.

I imagine a horror movie in which "All I Have to Do Is Dream" plays as a character slowly rounds a corner and finds a working jukebox in an abandoned restaurant. The Everly Brothers' melancholy, sweet voices waft from stereo speakers before a door opens to a showdown.

I download a dream app and read strangers' dreams. The matter-of-fact tone in the posts suggests a convincing near-reality; even the most absurd dreams sound real. As if they were always there, waiting for sleep to peel back and reveal them.

I dreamt that I was in my room, taking care of my 17 pet lizards. 12 were bearded dragons & 5 were geckos. I don't own any lizards[4]

The posts expose hidden lives for people who seem less like strangers as I read their dreams. I like the strange nonlinear dreams fixed on an object or landscape; dreams in fluid other worlds like ink pressed around stencil curves, through silk mesh, to convey an image. Or a needle stitching an image into eternity across skin.

*

My mother, sister, and I drove to visit my grandmother while she recovered from a procedure to address complications from systemic scleroderma. Staples like ladder rungs climbed an incision on my grandmother's torso. Beside her bed, a pale and earthy scent pulled on my ribs, my throat.

Doctors notified my aunt one evening that my grandmother was unlikely to live through the night. My aunt drove to the hospital to sit with my grandmother. Asleep, awake, the minutes blurred like hazy film.

My aunt told my mother she woke to a shimmer in the air, gold dust floating above the bed. She believes the gold dust was my grandmother's soul leaving her body.

*

I remember dying compared to going to sleep forever when I was younger.

Research shows slivers of other realms. Nodes affixed to a sleeping forehead, careful incisions on cadavers. A needle inking charts to reflect the brain's sleep activity, tissue and organs pushed aside with cold instruments to determine cause and time of death.

In 1907, physician Duncan MacDougall published findings from his 21 grams experiment. He weighed people before and after they died to determine if souls had physical weight, in addition to metaphorical heft.

And when they all were seated,/A Service, like a Drum –/Kept beating – beating – till I thought/My mind was going numb –

Emily Dickinson's "I felt a Funeral, in my Brain," concludes: *And then a Plank in Reason, broke,/And I dropped down, and down –/And hit a World, at every plunge,/And Finished knowing – then –*[5]

The woman on the television falls through the floors of her life. Each floor shows a different experience of sleep paralysis. Her episodes manifested as encounters with a terrifying ghost, who she called the Bent-Neck Lady. When the woman dies, she sees she has haunted herself all along. The ghost she feared while growing up foretold her suicide, her own bent neck. The shape in the dark she feared most was her future dead self.

In the 1990s, scientist Dr. Konstantin Korotkov tried to photograph the soul leaving the body. A stock photo shows this departure as a series of gold-green, person-shaped forms ascending from a body at rest. A supposedly authentic photo from the experiment resembles a color-mapped medical scan, a person's outline in triple. Different hues show body temperature before, during, and after death. A change in color marks a temperature shift, which supposedly indicates the soul exiting the body. The experiment did not show where the soul went, only its parting.

The beliefs that informed someone's understanding of a soul determined where the soul went.

One origin of the word *soul*: *Sometimes said to mean originally "coming from or belonging to the sea," because that was supposed to be the stopping place of the soul before birth or after death...*

The U.S. Geological Survey website states: *Up to 60% of the human adult body is water.*[6] I think of this whenever I try to drink more water. Or when I swim. Or when I read news of a drowning. We swallow what fills us. What fills us takes us back.

Consider the horizon early explorers regarded as the end of the world. Consider a man staring at the ocean, his horizon—a line he sees clearly—stretching horizontally. To every other person with him on beach chairs and plush towels warm in the sand, the line is a distant, hazy event they need not yet consider.

18.

I look for animals by the gorge. We are any couple at the park on a sunny afternoon, sipping ice cream coffee drinks until the cups echo wet-hollow. We decide to see a movie. Dave calls it *a fun one*—actors play actors and '50s filmmakers in Hollywood. There's an elaborate aqua musical number, a tap dance in a pub, a Western outpost serenade by moonlight.

We are recalibrating. He and I have not changed and everything feels altered. I am surprised by how infrequently we cry, how easy the everyday resumes and keeps happening. The shift is so subtle I'm taken aback at any reminder his father has died.

The next weekend, a man in a suit washed ashore on a beach sends a "suicide" whisper echoing through my head. Melancholy bookends the jokes, the *Jurassic Park* theme song hummed like a church hymn, slow-motion flashbacks in golden-hour light, a bus cobbled together from forest materials.

I brought a backpack filled with books to the Outer Banks the summer before. Among them, the issue of *POETRY* with Jenny Zhang's essay, "How It Feels," which I re-read every few days the summer following my uncle's death. I felt heavy and raw. The essay was a buoy.

Darkness is acceptable and even attractive so long as there is a threshold that is not crossed. But most people I know who suffer, suffer relentlessly and unendingly no matter what sort of future is proposed ("it'll get better/it won't always be like this/you will start to heal/I know it's such a cliché but you really will come out of this stronger in the end").[1]

*

I bake a flourless chocolate cake to take to our friends' house for dinner. Walking home, the sidewalk and streets are misty. Dave and I point at house after house. We say, *That one* and *That one* and *That one*, suggesting which we want to buy someday.

We watch a movie about criminals laying low in a picturesque Belgian city as they await their boss's next orders. I fall asleep wanting to travel to dreamy cities and mope beside pretty rivers, to eat beautiful, sweet confections. I fall asleep aching at the look on a man's face before he shoots himself and falls dead in the street: *You've got to stick to your principles.*[2]

Dave calls me home from work the next day. His father has died, he has to leave. Friends bring over Thai takeout for dinner. Everything happens fast until I walk our dog before bed and everything slows down slightly and the sky looks big. The afternoon rain has lifted and the sky is clearer. A friend takes me to the grocery store on St. Patrick's Day. Other years, I've bought corned beef and cabbage, soda bread in bags with shamrocks printed on the cellophane. I buy rice and lettuce and eggplant, prepared sushi and chocolate.

Invited to a pizza night, how much I talk embarrasses and surprises me. I talk as if I fear all the memories of someone go with them, as if I won't remember if I don't say it all in this instant. I go from present to past—Dave's flight, the family photo on the beach, my in-laws hugging Dave and me after our wedding reception, how loved and safe I felt. I eat until I can't eat any more.

At a restaurant the next night, I hardly touch what is before me because the group is large. I struggle to focus on what anyone says. I take my food home and eat while watching something I've already seen. A friend brings pastries and banana-flavored beer. I open one to see if I can taste the fruit and this is a short distraction.

We're given chicken and risotto the evening Dave returns. He and I are so hungry, we sit on the gold couch and eat directly from the Tupperware. It feels as if we have been apart longer than a week, like a thick curtain has been drawn between us. The meal puts us on the same horizon, a similar plane, even if what we each see is vastly different.

Little feels as certain as knowing we will never see his father again. Not because this is the only true thing, but because the idea of never seeing someone again is all-consuming. The thought repeats itself as if to cement an acceptance of the physical and abstract—death and grief, a colossal shifting. Eating, like other everyday tasks—bathing, dressing, telling time—is an afterthought, not a burden or enormous undertaking, but something that occurs to me secondarily. Hunger cramps my middle an hour after a hard cry.

Eating reminds me of daily routines, whether a favorite recipe or a new taste. Whether enormous joy, mammoth grief, or everyday occasions. We are born and someone feeds us. We gather and eat. Alone, we feed ourselves. We die and the people we leave eat what is offered. Wedding receptions. Post-funeral lunches. A mundane workday, snapping a lid from a container at a desk.

The note beneath the sandwich in a lunch bag. The crusts cut off. The chocolate bar I bought and remembered to bring. A meal softens solitude's sharp corners, illuminates cycles. A seed becomes a tomato. Dough becomes a medley of imperfect shapes that swell and float in boiling water. The shapes emerge pillowy. The ridges catch the sauce.

It felt like hearing a secret to learn the Wallace Stevens poem "The Emperor of Ice-Cream" is about preparing ice cream for a wake.

Chicken-wing delivery arrives in a Styrofoam box with the restaurant logo raised across the lid. Dave is at band practice in New York City. I'm with the pets for the night, reminded of apartments I lived in on my own. I love being alone, the privacy and quiet; I don't like feeling lonely. Our animals crowd me for the food. The dog drools on my foot. Each cat perches on a couch arm. I pull the coffee table to the sofa. Tangy hot sauce steams out the box vents. I watch the Bettie Page biopic. I watch Lifetime movies. I pull and bite the skin and meat, my fingers sticky. I suck the bones. I climb into bed feeling full.

*

The home insurance agent across the desk asks if we can name everything in our apartment, everything we own. Dave and I look at each other, waiting for the other to start naming belongings. The agent says to make a list, take pictures, note serial numbers, in case we ever need to replace our things. *It's harder than most people think*, she says. She tells us a story about a customer who called, frantic, when her family returned home from vacation to find the beds stripped and property missing. Burglars had collected the family's things in the bedding. The customer studied dust patterns on mantels and shelves to identify what was missing.

Think of an inventory of every meal you have ever eaten, every garment you have ever worn. Think of an index of all the things you have watched.

*

I remember some movies by their covers, a flicker of recognition, followed by blankness. Others I recall entire scenes, dialogue sprawls etched so clearly in my mind, watching them seems like reliving a recent conversation, even if years have passed.

*

Someone once described writing as going into a room each day and making choices. Some mornings, writing is like trying to fill graves that are sieves. Some mornings, I feel like I'm trying to write people back from the dead. I'm trying to write my own self back.

Frank Stanford was the first poet I read in grad school. This seemed like eerie fate to me. His poems are among the most alive I've ever read, like foreboding, wondrous letters. They tell me what I can only guess to know.

Steve Stern concludes a tribute to the poet, who ended his life at age twenty-nine: *In his poetry Frank Stanford travelled back and forth between life and death as if passing from one room to another. Two decades ago he went into one of the farthest rooms and locked the door behind him. That is not to say he abandoned the house.*[3]

Stanford still moves *back and forth between life and death*, speaking of the inevitable—what some deeply fear and dread, what some secretly long for.

I used to have less of an idea how much creative time may be lost to a sustained, ongoing pain, the wide, distracting shadow.

Some write from the darkness and back into it. I am swimming away. I am staring into the water. I am making this a buoy.

*

Some bridges have nets beneath them. Some mottos make me wish I lived some place else. Some years I was a cut. I was not the knife. I have felt the future closing in instead of expanding. I have imagined days and nights tilting forward without me. Overwhelmed by blankness. Like a street during a snowstorm.

*

There are worse things to talk about than weather.

Some days I believe I'm prepared for someone else who decides to leave the room. I am not prepared at all. The doors open and shut. Some places give no choice; some doors must close before the next will open. Some people talk about willpower or the will of God. They say, *I will* or *I will not*. They ask, *Will you?*

A woman walks into the woods, a dove balanced on her hand. She wears a long nightgown that flows around her like a sea. She wears a mask over her face—perfect features, a kind expression. She is quiet and hesitant, but curious about the night and trees. Each step is slow and new, yet cautious. She could almost be a ghost if this story started with someone finding her on the road. She could almost look like anyone else, except for her face, the mask.

Was it wind I meant? Have my parents told the Four-Day Win story wrong all these years? Something I saw that no one else could. Something knocked through my nightmares and tore the roof off our house, broke clean through sleep's fabric to emerge on this side.

A wind can comfort or chill, change or disappear. Absent electricity, felled trees, downed power lines, food spoiling in a warming refrigerator. A win can be held: medals, blue satin ribbon with foil stamping, trophies. I staged imaginary pageants in my playroom after my mom stopped signing me up for real ones. I put on a dress and pulled my trophies from the shelf with snow globes and fancy lady figurines. Small plaques read *Runner Up* and *Best Attire*. I pretended I had won, clutched each trophy to my chest, smiling wide. I waved slowly, like Miss America, to an audience of stuffed animals and dolls, my fingers pressed to crenulations, my hand a shell.

*

Nearly a year after his father dies, I help Dave deactivate his father's Facebook account. On the *Reason for leaving* list, he clicks the bubble for *Other, please explain further.* The list does not include a bubble for a death where someone organized their life into a binder: instructions, lists, passwords. *This is temporary. I'll be back* is an option on the screen, but we know it isn't really.

We are all temporary. We are all eternally cached.

In the *Other* box, beside instructions to explain, Dave types: *I am dead.*

*

We go for a walk at the Mulholland Wildflower Preserve. My last time walking here was with a friend, everyone on the path was talking about an election. It felt like a psychological thriller in which everyone is running away from the same horrible thing. So many of us moving in the same direction. Some of us coming back, warning, *There's no way out, we're stuck.* Heading back to my friend's house, we saw a deer eating foliage in golden-hour light.

Dave and I walk over a bridge above Van Natta Dam. Rushing beneath us are Wells Falls, also known as Businessman's Lunch Falls because businessmen eat lunch there. We see swimmers and sunbathers, no businessmen. Across the street, we enter the preserve.

In August 1998, Syracuse saw what became known as the Labor Day Storm, a thunderstorm so severe it was said a tornado touched down at the city's fairgrounds off I-690.

A highway of pipe runs along the walking path, like a giant metal earthworm tattooed in graffiti, muddy shoeprints, and scratches. The metal is strong enough to resist dents and gouges.

When I woke during the Labor Day Storm, I thought of *Fantasia*, the animated bacchanal segment. Baby unicorns learn to fly. Centaurs apply makeup and style anadems in their hair. They pair off and ride floral garland swings. Zeus disrupts the party when he parts the storm clouds overhead to throw lightning bolts down on the creatures, including Dionysus and his sad, drunk donkey.

The preserve thrives, abundant in life and death. The thought and the pipe stir a similar feeling; each startles at first, an intrusion that becomes part of the scenery. The pipe emerges and goes back underground along the trail, rising from the earth like a reminder before disappearing again. Like ancient sea monster drawings, scaly crescents arcing from waves and dipping back into the water. Like a plastic hand reaching from Halloween decorations, or a hand bursting from soil in a movie, the dead returning to life.

Walking back to the car, I think of animals. Deer, birds, raccoons, wandered-off housecats. I think of creatures I'm not seeing, those watching me and those who became part of the wildflowers and foliage.

I don't recall hearing about the storm before it happened, which sounds strange—as if a storm is expected to announce itself ahead of time. Before I went to bed, the wind didn't feel or smell any different, but I may not have been paying attention to it. I may not have known how yet. I sometimes miss believing dying meant going to sleep forever and thunder meant angels bowling in Heaven.

Consider again early explorers, the horizon they saw, the end of the world. The deeply held belief that to sail too far on a map meant to fall off the edge of Earth and die. Consider a waterfall that looks like the world falls off and ends.

I got out of bed, dragging my comforter behind me. I hid with our cat in my mother's closet. Studying weather in school, I'd learned a storm cellar or basement were ideal places to shelter during a severe storm, but a shower, doorjamb, or closet could do in a pinch. I fell asleep on the closet floor. I woke in morning. The sky was gray out the window. Torn leaves and branches littered the parking lot. Nested in the grass like a huge broken Easter egg, an uprooted celery-green power box. My mother was in our small kitchen, a cooler opened beside the fridge, lamenting the power outage and deciding which food she might save.

The preserve air smells of dirt and green leaves shaking on trees. As far back as we can walk on the path, two small waterfalls, a pool between them. The pipe runs submerged through the water. I want to swim across, go all the way under and come up for air behind the far waterfall so that it shimmers before me like a sheet—a veil between waking and sleep, life and death, fabric between bodies, the shroud between body and dirt, turf sheets dividing mourners from an open grave.

The word for what happened is *derecho*—a large, fast-moving complex of thunderstorms with powerful straight-line winds that cause widespread destruction. As in, derechos tore through Syracuse and several other cities the night I woke in the bedroom my sister and I shared. I parted the plastic blind slats. Rain fell in sheets, overwhelmed the apartment complex parking lot. Trees whipped their branches, twigs snapped off. The lightning like something I'd only seen in movies. Electric and pretty, thrumming veins, pink and green jagged streaks. It moved me; so many rickety ladders from earth to sky, each rung twisted and charged with volts, so violent and close.

Works Referenced

1000 Ways to Die. Dir. Will Raee, Tom McMahon. 2008–2012.

"280. I felt a Funeral, in my Brain." *The Complete Poems of Emily Dickinson*. Emily Dickinson. 1961.

The Adventures of Milo and Otis. Dir. Masanori Hata. 1989.

Almost Famous. Dir. Cameron Crowe. 2000.

The Babadook. Dir. Jennifer Kent. 2014.

Balto. Dir. Simon Wells. 1995.

Beetlejuice. Dir. Tim Burton. 1988.

"The Bent-Neck Lady." *The Haunting of Hill House*. Dir. Mike Flanagan. 2018.

The Cabin in the Woods. Dir. Drew Goddard. 2012.

Carrie. Dir. Brian De Palma. 1976.

"The Caterpillar." *Night Gallery*. Dir. Timothy Galfas and Jeannot Szwarc. Written by Rod Serling and Oscar Cook. 1972.

Clash of the Titans. Dir. Desmond Davis. 1981.

"Congress." *The Visiting Privilege: New and Collected Stories*. Joy Williams. 2015.

Creature from the Black Lagoon. Dir. Jack Arnold. 1954.

"Dark Paradise." *Born To Die*. Lana Del Rey. 2012.

Darkness Falls. Dir. Jonathan Liebesman. 2003.

"Dear David: Documenting the ghost in my apartment." Adam Ellis. https://wakelet.com/wake/e6275d03-7bce-4789-9961-f3a04723cc71.

The Descent. Dir. Neil Marshall. 2006.

"Dire Wolf." *Trouble in Mind*. Lucie Brock-Broido. 2005.

"'Dog Suicide Bridge': Why Do So Many Pets Keep Leaping Into a Scottish Gorge?" Ceylan Yeginsu. *The New York Times*, March 27, 2019. https://www.nytimes.com/2019/03/27/world/europe/scotland-overtoun-bridge-dog-suicide.html.

"Doug's Nightmare on Jumbo Street." *Doug*. Jim Jinkins & Joe Fallon. 1993.

Dreamcatcher. Dir. Lawrence Kasdan. 2003.

"Egyptian Book of the Dead." Joshua J. Mark. *Ancient History Encyclopedia*. https://www.ancient.eu/Egyptian_Book_of_the_Dead/.

"The Emperor of Ice-Cream." *The Collected Poems of Wallace Stevens*. Wallace Stevens. 1954.

Evil Dead II. Dir. Sam Raimi. 1987.

Eyes Without a Face. Dir. Georges Franju. 1962.

Faces of Death. Dir. John Alan Schwartz. 1978.

Fantasia. Dir. Samuel Armstrong, James Algar, Bill Roberts. 1940.

The Fly. Dir. David Cronenberg. 1986.

"Four Ways to Survive a Coyote Attack." Wikihow. https://www.wikihow.com/Survive-a-Coyote-Attack.

The Four-Day Win: End Your Diet War and Achieve Thinner Peace. Martha Beck. 2006.

"Frank Stanford: An Appreciation." *Hidden Water: From the Frank Stanford Archives*. Steven Stern. 2015.

"from *Microliths*." Paul Celan. Translated by Pierre Joris. *POETRY Magazine*, January 2017.

Giselle. Libretto by Jules-Henri Vernoy de Saint-Georges, Théophile Gautier. Music composed by Adolphe Adam. 1841.

The Good Funeral: Death, Grief, and the Community of Care. Thomas Lynch and Thomas G. Long. 2013.

"Grand Unified Theory of Female Pain." *The Empathy Exams.* Leslie Jamison. 2014.

Hail, Caesar! Dir. Ethan Coen & Joel Coen. 2016.

The Haunting of Hill House. Shirley Jackson. 1959.

"Here's How to Keep Your Cat Forever." Molly Oswaks. *The New York Times*, 13 Jan. 2020. https://www.nytimes.com/2020/01/13/style/self-care/etsy-death-pet.html.

Hostel. Dir. Eli Roth. 2006.

House of 1000 Corpses. Dir. Rob Zombie. 2003.

The House of the Devil. Dir. Ti West. 2009.

House of Wax. Dir. Jaume Collet-Serra. 2005.

"How It Feels." Jenny Zhang. *POETRY Magazine*, July/August 2015.

"How to Kill Tree of Heaven the Organic Way!" BroBryceGardens Youtube Channel, 2014. https://www.youtube.com/watch?v=iD3h-4BlbYE&t=26s.

How to Lose a Guy in 10 Days. Dir Donald Petrie. 2003.

"I had 17 lizards." sailortabbycat. Dream Journal Ultimate App, Dream Wall. Aug. 7, 2017.

In Bruges. Dir. Martin McDonagh. 2008.

Inferno. Dir. Dario Argento. 1980.

It Follows. Dir. David Robert Mitchell. 2015.

Jaws. Dir. Steven Spielberg. 1975.

Job, bronze sculpture. Ivan Meštrović. 1945.

Kedi. Dir. Ceyda Torun. 2017.

The Kittens' Wedding. Walter Potter. 1890. Displayed at The Morbid Anatomy Museum during the "Taxidermy: Art, Science, & Immortality" exhibit, Fall 2016.

The Last House on the Left. Dir. Wes Craven. 1972.

Little Shop of Horrors. Dir. Frank Oz. 1986.

Lost River. Dir. Ryan Gosling. 2015.

The Making of 'JAWS.' Dir. Laurent Bouzereau. 1995.

Misery. Dir. Rob Reiner. 1990.

Morbid Anatomy Museum, https://www.morbidanatomy.org/blog.

"Mourn You Better." *Bone Confetti*. Muriel Leung. 2016.

Museum of Death, www.museumofdeath.net.

The Night of the Hunter. Dir. Charles Laughton. 1955.

A Nightmare on Elm Street. Dir. Wes Craven. 1984.

"Nightmare on Evergreen Terrace: Treehouse of Horror VI." *The Simpsons*. Bob Anderson & Steve Tompkins. 1995.

"The Nocturnal Ships of the Past." *The Singing Knives*. Frank Stanford. 2008.

"Now." *The Incognito Lounge*. Denis Johnson. 2007.

"On Sentimentality." *Madness, Rack, and Honey: Collected Lectures*. Mary Ruefle. 2012.

"On the Non-Denial Denial of Death." *The Morbid Anatomy Anthology*. John Troyer. 2014.

Pet Sematary. Dir. Mary Lambert. 1989.

Poltergeist. Dir. Tobe Hooper. 1982.

A Quiet Place. Dir. John Krasinski. 2018.

Raw. Dir. Julia Ducournau. 2016.

Return to Oz. Dir. Walter Murch. 1985.

Revenge. Dir. Coralie Fargeat. 2018.

The Ring. Dir. Gore Verbinski. 2002.

Romeo and Juliet. Libretto based on William Shakespeare's *Romeo and Juliet*. Music composed by Sergei Prokofiev. 1935.

Rosemary's Baby. Dir. Roman Polanski. 1968.

"Ruage." Aase Berg. *Surrealist Group of Stockholm*, Number 4, March 1996. http://surrealistgruppen.org/ruage.html.

Save Our Cemeteries (New Orleans), www.saveourcemeteries.org.

Scream. Dir. Wes Craven. 1996.

Se7en. Dir. David Fincher. 1995.

Seneca White Deer, www.senecawhitedeer.org.

"Sharks and Suicide." *Ill Nature: Rants and Reflections on Humanity and Other Animals*. Joy Williams. 2002.

The Shining. Dir. Stanley Kubrick. 1980.

"Six Months after Contemplating Suicide." *Lessons on Expulsion*. Erika L. Sánchez. 2017.

Smoke Gets in Your Eyes: And Other Lessons from the Crematory. Caitlin Doughty. 2015.

"Snow." *Actual Air*. David Berman. 1999.

"The Soul: Hypothesis Concerning Soul Substance Together with Experimental Evidence of the Existence of Such Substance." Duncan MacDougall. *American Medicine*. 1907.

Supplicant Persephone, bronze sculpture. Ivan Meštrović. 1945.

Suspiria. Dir. Dario Argento. 1977.

Suspiria. Dir. Luca Guadagnino. 2018.

Swan Lake. Music composed by Pyotr Ilyich Tchaikovsky. 1875.

Swiss Army Man. Dir. Daniel Kwan & Daniel Scheinert. 2016.

La Sylphide. Libretto by Adolphe Nourrit. Music composed by Jean-Madeleine Schneitzhoeffer. 1832.

Taxidermy Art: A Rogue's Guide to the Work, the Culture, and How to Do It Yourself. Robert Marbury. 2014.

Teeth. Dir. Mitchell Lichtenstein. 2007.

The Texas Chain Saw Massacre. Dir. Tobe Hooper. 1974.

The Texas Chainsaw Massacre 2. Dir. Tobe Hooper. 1986.

Titanic. Dir. James Cameron. 1997.

Toddlers and Tiaras, TLC, 2009–2016.

Traces of Death. Written by Damon Fox. 1993.

True Detective. Written by Nic Pizzolatto, Dir. Cary Joji Fukunaga. 2014.

Twin Peaks: Fire Walk with Me. Dir. David Lynch. 1992.

"UAV Drone video of Loss Lake Split Rock Quarry Camillus NY." RMS Video YouTube Channel. 2016. https://www.youtube.com/watch?v=k2FPbYKZYq8.

ViaGen Pets, viagenpets.com.

The Virgin Spring. Dir. Ingmar Bergman. 1960.

"Wait." *Mortal Acts, Mortal Words*. Galway Kinnell. 1980.

"The Water in You: Water and the Human Body." U.S. Geological Survey. https://www.usgs.gov/special-topic/water-science-school/science/water-you-water-and-human-body?qt-science_center_objects=0#qt-science_center_objects.

What Ever Happened to Baby Jane? Dir. Robert Aldrich. 1962.

Where the Red Fern Grows. Rawls Wilson. 1961.

"Why is a funeral director called an undertaker?" Grammarphobia. January 2007. https://www.grammarphobia.com/blog/2007/01/why-is-a-funeral-director-called-an-undertaker.html.

Wild Things. Dir. John McNaughton. 1998.

The Wizard of Oz. Dir. Victor Fleming, George Cukor, Mervyn LeRow, Norman Taurog. 1939.

WSTM Channel 3 News, "Camillus Mall," 1986. Syracuse Nostalgia YouTube Channel, 2009. https://www.youtube.com/watch?v=vWaH8lGowwI&t=41s.

Definitions & Etymological References

Definitions collaged into the text are from Merriam-Webster's Online Dictionary and Dictionary.com. Etymological references are from Douglas Harper's *Online Etymology Dictionary* (www.etymonline.com). Harper's project draws on a wealth of linguistic sources to index word origins online.

Notes

1.

[1] Syracuse Nostalgia, "WSTM Channel 3 News—Camillus Mall —1986 NY," YouTube, Mar 6, 2009, https://www.youtube.com/watch?v=vWaH8lGowwI.

[2] Craven, Wes (Director), *Scream*, Dimension Films, 1996.

[3] Bouzereau, Laurent (Director), *The Making of Jaws*, MCA/Universal Home Video, 1995.

2.

[1] Williams, Joy. "Sharks and Suicide." *Ill Nature: Rants and Reflections on Humanity and Other Animals* (New York: Vintage, 2002), 92.

[2] Ibid.

[3] Ibid., 93.

[4] Spielberg, Steven (Director), *Jaws*, Universal Pictures, 1975.

3.

[1] Collet-Serra, Jaume (Director), *House of Wax*, Warner Bros. Pictures, 2005.

[2] Aldrich, Robert (Director), *What Ever Happened to Baby Jane?*, Warner Bros. Pictures, 1962.

4.

[1] Burton, Tim (Director), *Beetlejuice*, Warner Bros. Pictures, 1988.

[2] Zhang, Jenny. "How It Feels." *POETRY Magazine*, July/August 2015.

[3] Burton, *Beetlejuice.*

[4] Hooper, Tobe (Director), *Poltergeist*, MGM/UA Entertainment Company, 1982.

[5] Lynch, Thomas and Long, Thomas G. *The Good Funeral: Death, Grief, and the Community of Care* (Westminster John Knox, 2013), 202.

[6] Hooper, *Poltergeist.*

[7] Verbinski, Gore (Director), *The Ring*, DreamWorks Pictures, 2002.

5.

[1] Del Rey, Lana, "Dark Paradise," *Born to Die*, Interscope Records, 2012.

[2] Johnson, Denis. "Now." *The Incognito Lounge* (Pittsburgh: Carnegie Mellon University Press, 2007), 40.

[3] Celan, Paul. "from *Microliths.*" Translated by Pierre Joris. *POETRY Magazine*, January 2017.

[4] Marshall, Neil (Director), *The Descent*, Lionsgate, 2002.

6.

[1] Mitchell, David Robert (Director), *It Follows*, RADiUS-TWC, 2015.

[2] Ibid.

[3] Berman, David. "Snow." *Actual Air* (Open City Books, 1999), 5.

[4] Mitchell, *It Follows.*

[5] Dostoevsky, Fyodor. Translated by Constance Garnett. *The Idiot* (New York: The Macmillan Company, 1915), 62.

[6] Stanford, Frank. "The Nocturnal Ships of the Past." *The Singing Knives* (Lost Roads, 2008), 27.

7.

[1] Heine, Heinrich. *De l'Allemagne*, French edition, 1835, as cited in Beaumont, Cyril William. *The Ballet Called Giselle* (United Kingdom: C. W. Beaumont, 1944) 19.

[2] Guadagnino, Luca (Director), *Suspiria*, Amazon Studios, 2018.

[3] West, Ti (Director), *The House of the Devil*, MPI Media Group, 2009.

[4] Ibid.

[5] Polanski, Roman (Director), *Rosemary's Baby*, Paramount Pictures, 1968.

[6] Kent, Jennifer (Director), *The Babadook*, IFC Films, 2014.

[7] Ibid.

8.

[1] Lichtenstein, Mitchell (Director), *Teeth*, Roadside Attractions, 2007.

[2] Sánchez, Erika L. "Six Months after Contemplating Suicide." *Lessons on Expulsion* (Minneapolis: Graywolf, 2017), 72.

[3] De Palma, Brian (Director), *Carrie*, United Artists, 1976.

[4] Jamison, Leslie. "Grand Unified Theory of Female Pain." *The Empathy Exams* (Minneapolis: Graywolf, 2014), 218.

[5] De Palma, *Carrie*.

9.

[1] Berg, Aase. "Ruage." Surrealist Group of Stockholm, Number 4, March 1996. http://surrealistgruppen.org/ruage.html.

[2] Ibid.

10.

[1] Lynch, David (Director), *Twin Peaks: Fire Walk with Me*, Warner Bros. Pictures, 1992.

[2] Ibid.

[3] Zombie, Rob (Director), *House of 1000 Corpses*, Lionsgate, 2003.

[4] Ducournau, Julia (Director), *Raw*, Focus World, 2016.

[5] Lynch, *Twin Peaks: Fire Walk with Me*.

11.

[1] Seneca White Deer, www.senecawhitedeer.org.

[2] Powe, J. D. & Evan Michelson. Curatorial statement displayed at the Morbid Anatomy Museum's "Taxidermy: Art, Science, & Immortality" exhibit, Fall 2016.

[3] Ibid.

[4] Lambert, Mary (Director), *Pet Sematary*, Paramount Pictures, 1989.

12.

[1] Celan, "from *Microliths*."

13.

[1] Museum of Death, www.museumofdeath.net.

[2] Save Our Cemeteries (New Orleans), www.saveourcemeteries.org.

[3] Berg, "Ruage."

[4] Leung, Muriel. "Mourn You Better." *Bone Confetti* (Las Cruces: Noemi Press, 2016), 4.

[5] Ibid., 58.

⁶ Mitchell, *It Follows*.

⁷ Morbid Anatomy Museum, https://www.morbidanat-omy.org/blog.

⁸ Marbury, Robert. *Taxidermy Art: A Rogue's Guide to the Work, the Culture, and How to Do It Yourself* (New York: Artisan, 2014), 12.

⁹ Williams, Joy. "Congress." *The Visiting Privilege: New and Collected Stories* (New York: Alfred A. Knopf, 2015), 255.

¹⁰ Zhang, "How It Feels."

¹¹ "Form and Void." *True Detective*. Nic Pizzolatto (Writer), Cary Joji Fukunaga (Director), HBO, 2014.

¹² Goddard, Drew (Director), *The Cabin in the Woods*, Lionsgate, 2012.

¹³ Raimi, Sam (Director), *Evil Dead II*, De Laurentiis Entertainment Group, 1987.

14.

¹ Yeginsu, Ceylan. "'Dog Suicide Bridge': Why Do So Many Pets Keep Leaping Into a Scottish Gorge?" *The New York Times*, March 27, 2019. https://www.nytimes.com/2019/03/27/world/europe/scotland-overtoun-bridge-dog-suicide.html.

² Spielberg, *Jaws*.

³ "Four Ways to Survive a Coyote Attack." Wikihow, https://www.wikihow.com/Survive-a-Coyote-Attack#.

⁴ "Doug's Nightmare on Jumbo Street." *Doug*, Joe Fallon (Writer), Carol Millican, Yvette Kaplan (Directors), Nickelodeon, 1993.

15.

1 Brock-Broido, Lucie. "Dire Wolf." *Trouble in Mind* (New York: Alfred A. Knopf, 2005), 66.

2 "Why is a funeral director called an undertaker?" Grammarphobia, https://www.grammarphobia.com/blog/2007/01/why-is-a-funeral-director-called-an-undertaker.html, January 2007.

3 Troyer, John. "Funeral Planning Worksheet from Bath Centre for Death and Society." Included in "On the Non-Denial Denial of Death." Ebenstein, Joanna and Dickey, Colin (Editors)*The Morbid Anatomy Anthology* (Brooklyn: Morbid Anatomy Press, 2014), 453.

16.

1 Ruefle, Mary. "On Sentimentality." *Madness, Rack, and Honey: Collected Lectures* (Seattle and New York: Wave Books, 2012), 51.

2 Kinnell, Galway. "Wait." *Mortal Acts, Mortal Words* (New York: Houghton Mifflin, 1980), 15.

3 Mark, Joshua J. "Egyptian Book of the Dead." Ancient History Encyclopedia. https://www.ancient.eu/Egyptian_Book_of_the_Dead/.

4 Jackson, Shirley (Author), Oates, Joyce Carol (Editor), *Novels and Stories: The Lottery, The Haunting of Hill House, We Have Always Lived in the Castle, other stories and sketches* (Library of America, 2010), 270.

17.

1 Craven, Wes (Director), *A Nightmare on Elm Street*, New Line Cinema, 1984.

2 Ibid.

[3] Shakespeare, William. *Hamlet.*

[4] sailortabbycat. "I had 17 lizards." Dream Journal Ultimate App, Dream Wall. Aug 7, 2017.

[5] Dickinson, Emily (Author), Johnson, Thomas H. (Editor) "280. I felt a Funeral, in my Brain." *The Complete Poems of Emily Dickinson* (Boston: Little, Brown and Company, 1961), 129.

[6] "The Water in You: Water and the Human Body." U.S. Geological Survey. https://www.usgs.gov/special-topic/water-science-school/science/water-you-water-and-human-body?qt-science_center_objects=0#qt-science_center_objects.

18.

[1] Zhang, "How It Feels."

[2] McDonagh, Martin (Director), *In Bruges*, Focus Features, 2008.

[3] Stern, Steven. "Frank Stanford: An Appreciation." *Hidden Water: From the Frank Stanford Archives* (Nashville: Third Man Books, 2015), xiii.

Acknowledgements

I'm grateful to Eric and Eliza Obenauf, and everyone at Two Dollar Radio, for believing in this book.

To Chelsea Hodson, for your generous, thoughtful guidance.

To Jeannie Vanasco and Amy Berkowitz for sharing kind words.

To Bükem Reitmayer and Cosmonauts Avenue for publishing the essay which grew into this collection.

Enormous thanks, love, and appreciation to Jessica del Mundo, Jose Perez Beduya, Alexandra Chang, Kina Viola, Marty Cain, Jennifer Savran Kelly, Laurel O'Brien, JT Tompkins, and Kit Frick. To my family. To Hester, Rooney, and Myrtle. And last here, but first, each day, always, to Dave. For your love and generous mind, your light and support. All of it.

Two Dollar Radio
Books too loud to Ignore

ALSO AVAILABLE Here are some other titles you might want to dig into.

THE HARE NOVEL MELANIE FINN

← "[A] brooding feminist thriller." —*New York Times*

← "Finn has a gift for weaving existential and political concerns through tautly paced prose." —Molly Young, *Vulture*

AN ASTOUNDING NEW LITERARY THRILLER from a celebrated author at the height of her storytelling prowess, *The Hare* bravely considers a woman's inherent sense of obligation—sexual and emotional—to the male hierarchy.

TWO DOLLAR RADIO GUIDE TO NAMING YOUR BABY

WITH ALL THE SWAGGER of the Palmyra Pumpkin Princess, the Two Dollar Radio Guide to Naming Your Baby will help you name your child by calling attention to those names you should probably definitely avoid. While we can't promise your child will be a success, we can provide you with the tools necessary to ensure your child will not be an epic failure.

TWO DOLLAR RADIO GUIDE TO VEGAN COOKING

← "This cookbook is imaginative and creative while also featuring accessible vegan recipes that are both healthy (mostly) and just super delicious all around. Two thumbs way up, and all of my other fingers as well, for this creative little cookbook." —Audrey Farnsworth, *Fodor's Travel*

WE ARE ALL EXPLORERS, vegan food explorers—join us on this culinary journey as we slay Vegan Hunger Demons.

A HISTORY OF MY BRIEF BODY
ESSAYS BY BILLY-RAY BELCOURT

← "Stunning... Belcourt meditates on the difficulty and necessity of finding joy as a queer NDN in a country that denies that joy all too often... Happiness, this beautiful book says, is the ultimate act of resistance." —Michelle Hart, *O, The Oprah Magazine*

A BRAVE, RAW, AND fiercely intelligent collection of essays and vignettes on grief, colonial violence, joy, love, and queerness.

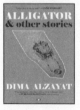

ALLIGATOR STORIES BY DIMA ALZAYAT

⇢ PEN/Robert W. Bingham Award for Debut Short Story Collection, longlist.
⇢ Swansea University Dylan Thomas Prize 2021, longlist.

← "A stellar debut... Alzayat manages to execute a short but thoughtful meditation on the spectrum of race in America from Jackson's presidency to present." —Colin Groundwater, *GQ*

THE AWARD-WINNING STORIES in Dima Alzayat's collection are luminous and tender, rich and relatable, chronicling a sense of displacement through everyday scenarios.

Books to read!

WHITEOUT CONDITIONS NOVEL BY **TARIQ SHAH**

← *"Whiteout Conditions* is both disorienting and visceral, hilarious and heartbreaking." —Michael Welch, *Chicago Review of Books*

IN THE DEPTHS OF A BRUTAL Midwest winter, Ant rides with Vince through the falling snow to Ray's funeral, an event that has been accruing a sense of consequence. With a poet's sensibility, Shah navigates the murky responsibilities of adulthood, grief, toxic masculinity, and the tragedy of revenge in this haunting Midwestern noir.

VIRTUOSO NOVEL BY **YELENA MOSKOVICH**

→ **Longlisted for the Swansea University Dylan Thomas Prize**

← "A bold feminist novel." —Katharine Coldiron, *Times Literary Supplement*

← *"Virtuoso* is powerfully mysterious and deeply insightful."
—Nadia Beard, *Los Angeles Review of Books*

WITH A DISTINCTIVE PROSE FLAIR and spellbinding vision, a story of love, loss, and self-discovery that heralds Yelena Moskovich as a brilliant and one-of-a-kind visionary.

SOME OF US ARE VERY HUNGRY NOW
ESSAYS BY **ANDRE PERRY**

→ **Best Books 2019:** *Pop Matters*

← "A complete, deep, satisfying read." —Gabino Iglesias, NPR

ANDRE PERRY'S DEBUT COLLECTION of personal essays travels from Washington DC to Iowa City to Hong Kong in search of both individual and national identity while displaying tenderness and a disarming honesty.

SAVAGE GODS MEMOIR BY **PAUL KINGSNORTH**

→ **A Best Book of 2019** —*The Guardian*

← "[*Savage Gods* is] a wail sent up from the heart of one of the intractable problems of the human condition: real change comes only from crisis, and crisis always involves loss."
—Ellie Robins, *Los Angeles Review of Books*

SAVAGE GODS ASKS, can words ever paint the truth of the world—or are they part of the great lie which is killing it?

THE BOOK OF X NOVEL BY **SARAH ROSE ETTER**

→ **Winner of the 2019 Shirley Jackson Awards for Novel**
→ **A Best Book of 2019** —*Vulture, Entropy, Buzzfeed, Thrillist*

← "Etter brilliantly, viciously lays bare what it means to be a woman in the world." —Roxane Gay

A SURREAL EXPLORATION OF ONE WOMAN'S LIFE and death against a landscape of meat, office desks, and bad men.

Thank you for supporting independent culture!
Feel good about yourself.

MAY 2021

Books to read!

Now available at **TWODOLLARRADIO.com** or your favorite bookseller.

TRIANGULUM NOVEL BY **MASANDE NTSHANGA**

→ **2020 Nomo Awards Shortlist**
→ **A Best Book of 2019** —*LitReactor, Entropy*

← "Magnificently disorienting and meticulously constructed."
—Tobias Carroll, Tor.com

AN AMBITIOUS, OFTEN PHILOSOPHICAL AND GENRE-BENDING NOVEL that covers a period of over 40 years in South Africa's recent past and near future.

THE WORD FOR WOMAN IS WILDERNESS
NOVEL BY **ABI ANDREWS**

← "Unlike any published work I have read, in ways that are beguiling, audacious…" —Sarah Moss, *The Guardian*

THIS IS A NEW KIND OF NATURE WRITING — one that crosses fiction with science writing and puts gender politics at the center of the landscape.

AWAY! AWAY! NOVEL BY **JANA BEŇOVÁ**
TRANSLATED BY **JANET LIVINGSTONE**

→ **Winner of the European Union Prize for Literature**

← "Beňová's short, fast novels are a revolution against normality."
—Austrian Broadcasting Corporation, ORF

WITH MAGNETIC, SPARKLING PROSE, Beňová delivers a lively mosaic that ruminates on human relationships, our greatest fears and desires.

THE DEEPER THE WATER THE UGLIER THE FISH NOVEL BY **KATYA APEKINA**

→ **2018 *Los Angeles Times* Book Prize Finalist**
→ **A Best Book of 2018** —*Kirkus, BuzzFeed, Entropy, LitReactor, LitHub*
← "Nothing short of gorgeous." —Michael Schaub, NPR

POWERFULLY CAPTURES THE QUIET TORMENT of two sisters craving the attention of a parent they can't, and shouldn't, have to themselves.

THE BLURRY YEARS NOVEL BY **ELEANOR KRISEMAN**

→ **A Best Book of 2018** —*Entropy*
← "Kriseman's is a new voice to celebrate."—*Publishers Weekly*

THE BLURRY YEARS IS A POWERFUL and unorthodox coming-of-age story from an assured new literary voice, featuring a stirringly twisted mother-daughter relationship, set against the sleazy, vividly-drawn backdrop of late-seventies and early-eighties Florida.

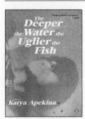